STORMTROOP

Also by Leo Kessler

Leo Kessler

Stormtroop

Futura Publications Limited
A Futura Book

A Futura Book

First published in Great Britain by
Futura Publications Limited in 1977

ISBN 0 8600 7550 8
Printed in Great Britain by
Hazell Watson and Viney Ltd
Aylesbury, Bucks

Futura Publications Limited
110 Warner Road, Camberwell
London S.E.5

CLASH ON MOUNT CLIDI

'Then let each man turn straight to the front
Come death, come life.
That's how war and battle kiss and prattle.'
The Iliad, Book XVII

SITUATION IN THE AEGEAN SEA
SEPTEMBER, 1943

Turkey

Lesbos

Samos

Leros

Kos

Rhodes

Carpathos

 German-held territory

Neutral-Turkish territory

 Italian-held territory

A MISSION IS PROPOSED

CHAPTER ONE

'Form up now!' Jellicoe ordered, his eyes directed at the dark horizon and not at the little fleet of ships ploughing steadily forward through the Aegean at ten knots an hour.

'Ay, ay, sir,' the bearded sergeant standing next to him on the bridge of the shabby converted Greek caique answered.

Jellicoe grinned. These days his Tommies of the Special Boat Service were more Navy than the Royal Navy itself.

Swiftly the sergeant flicked his Aldis lamp on and off. Each boat acknowledged in its turn and rapidly the ramshackle invasion fleet closed up. If there were going to be trouble, it would begin soon. Now they were only half an hour's sailing from the island.

On the horizon black rain clouds were beginning to build up and as yet there was no moon. But there was sufficient visibility from the first pale stars to make out the dark brown smudge of the island well enough and the mountain which dominated it.

Jellicoe, the Commander of the Special Boat Service, surveyed the silent island through his night glasses and said a silent prayer that the Italian gunners on top of that mountain would follow the example of their government in faraway Italy, which had surrendered to the Allies. If they didn't . . . hurriedly Jellicoe banished the thought. It didn't do to dwell on the guns too long.

'Signal the MTBs.* Come in close on port and starboard, signaller!' Jellicoe commanded.

'Ay, ay, sir,' the sergeant answered, as if he were some grizzled 'three-striper' with thirty years' naval service behind him, instead of being ex-salesman in ladies' lingerie who had gone to sea for the first time only a year before. Swiftly he went to work with his lamp. They were now

*Motor Torpedo Boats.

entering the final phase of the little invasion of this remote corner of the Aegean.

The young Commander crossed his fingers for luck, then looked around to see if any of his crew had spotted the schoolboy gesture. None had. He grinned and spat into the sea to complete the prep school ritual for appeasing the gods. Now there was nothing else he could do but hope.

In the MTBs, the young sailors prepared for action. In the gun turrets the gunners breathed on their spray-frozen fingers to warm them; the torpedomen checked the firing mechanisms once more; the signallers cradled their lamps ready to flash a signal to the unarmed caiques as soon as they sighted the enemy; and on the bridges, the young captains, their faces pale and sickly from the wild bucketing of the 70-foot boats at high speed searched the dark horizon for the Jerry S-boats which they knew were out there somewhere.

'*Sir!*' It was the forward look-out on *MTB 106*.

The 20-year-old skipper swung round. 'What?'

'Ship to port, sir!'

The captain focused his glasses in a frenzy of fumbling. A sinister, long hull slid into the circle of calibrated glass. Then another. '*S boats!*' he breathed to himself. German motor torpedo boats, some thousand yards outside the harbour of Portolago, clustered together as if they had stopped at some prearranged rendezvous. And as yet they had not spotted the invasion fleet creeping forward towards the island!

'Ahead port, ahead starboard!' he cried.

The tremendous 1,000 HP engines, which had been trembling at ten knots, exploded into life. Down below the Chief Motor Mechanic thrust the throttle levers forward. The silence was torn apart. Suddenly the bridge was flodded with the pungent stench of hot oil. In an instant the MTB's rakish bow lifted clean out of the water. Two wild white wings of water foamed high in the air at her stern. At thirty-five knots *MTB 106* seemed to be flying

10

above the sea, its lean outline silhouetted against the cascading water.

A thousand yards away, an urgent blue light winked on and off. The surprised S-boats were asking for identification. The skipper of the *106* ignored the challenge. *'Engage enemy!'* he commanded, his pale young face flushed with the excitement of battle.

The forward gunner was first to react. He swung his old-fashioned Lewis gun round. Green tracer arched towards the still motionless S-boats. Frantically the German sailors dashed to their posts to get the boats under way before it was too late. The skipper of *106* crouched over the torpedo sight. The leading S-boat was only 700 yards away now. He made a snap decision in case her captain managed to get her under way. He aimed his torpedo just ahead of her bows.

At Portolago, the one German-manned shore battery opened up. A star shell exploded above the MTBs, turning night into day. As it began to fade in a shower of sparklets, tracer zipped through the air towards the attackers. In white, green and red phosphor, it criss-crossed the sea like a myriad fireflies. Tensed over his sight, the young skipper could hear the frightening burr of angry metal tearing up the wood of the deck timbers. But he kept eyes fixed on the sight.

The leading S-boat, its engines already thundering, was 600 yards away now. On all sides the sea churned and frothed with falling 20mm shells from the shore battery. But *MTB 106* seemed to bear a charmed life. Heeling from side to side she came in for the kill.

At 500 yards, the skipper ripped back the torpedo firing lever. A dull clang. A hiss. The boat shuddered, as the torpedo, packed with two tons of high explosive, hit the water.

'Hard to starboard!' the skipper commanded above the snarl of machine-gun fire.

In a great flurry of white water, the MTB veered to starboard. In that same moment, there was a tremendous

11

explosion. The young skipper glanced over his shoulder. Where the leading S-boat had been, a huge sheet of flame had shot into the night air, colouring the low cloud an angry scarlet. He grinned and suddenly realized that his right shoulder hurt like hell; and there was something hot and wet trickling down his arm.

Now it was the turn of the other motor torpedo boat, *MTB 108*. Lewis gun blazing furiously, she zoomed in to the attack. The remaining S-boat had recovered from the surprise of the sudden assault. While her skipper tried desperately to get her under way, her gunner raked *MTB 108*'s superstructure with his twin Spandaus. At 800 rounds a minute, he hosed the speeding boat's deck. Glass shattered. Wood and metal splinters flew everywhere. Spent slugs whirred away into the glowing darkness. Ratings howled with agony and dropped to the battle-littered deck.

Blinded, frightened, bleeding from their wounds, the survivors raced into the whirling cone of red and white tracer. Crouched over the sight, the skipper ignored the mad world all around him, his eyes fixed hypnotically on the instrument. *One thousand yards . . . nine hundred . . . eight hundred . . .* Jaw clenched, every muscle taut with fright and tension, he prepared to fire . . . *Seven hundred yards . . .* The bucking, heaving little craft had reached the centre of the maelstrom now. She was ablaze from stem to stern, angry flames licking up around his feet, as his hand tightened around the firing lever . . . *Six hundred yards . . . five hundred and fifty . . .* The skipper opened his mouth automatically, ready for the blast which must soon come. *Five hundred.* NOW!

He jerked the firing lever and simultaneously screamed 'Hard to port!'

The dying helmsman swung the shattered wooden boat round an instant before he slumped to the deck, already sticky with the blood of those who had died before him.

Nothing! An age seemed to pass. Blindly the skipper

staggered to the controls, seeing nothing, hearing nothing, his whole being concentrated on what *had* to come.

Suddenly there was a sickening explosion which struck him like a physical blow in the pit of his stomach. He gasped painfully. Another blast hit him across the face like an open-handed blow. Behind him the S-boat disintegrated. Flaming wreckage sailed skywards, whirling wildly in a hundred different directions. As the skipper of the *MTB 108* slipped to the deck, his horrified eyes looking at the severed hand which lay on the shattered planks like a discarded white glove, he knew he had done it. The way was free.

'All right,' *MTB 106*'s captain muttered through gritted teeth, trying to ignore the burning pain in his wounded shoulder, 'signal his Lordship that he can take his bloody little kipper boxes in now!'
The invasion of the Island of Leros could begin!

TWO

Like flies crawling up the silver envelope of an airship, the tiny black dots laboured up the snow of the mighty mountain, 2,000 metres above sea-level. High above them the blue-white peak, their target this fine September day, seemed to taunt them to make that last, back-breaking effort to conquer it.

In the lead Colonel Stuermer, the C.O. of Stormtroop Edelweiss, the *Hochalpenkorps** elite reconnaissance and assault company, had his eyes everywhere. Twenty years of climbing everywhere in Europe, Asia and South America had taught him that eyes were more important than muscles. A leader must always be on the look-out, planning

*Literally 'High Alpine Corps', a designation given to that part of a wartime German Mountain Division capable of climbing above a certain height.

each new move even before the team had completed the one they were currently engaged on. His peaked cap, with the metal Edelweiss* badge of the Stormtroop on its side, set at a jaunty angle, a common soldier's carbine slung across his broad shoulders, he climbed effortlessly upwards although twice as old as most of his alpine troopers.

Behind him on the rope came Major Gottfried Greul, his second-in-command, climbing with that same brutal energetic zest which had made him the idol of the pre-war Hitler Youth and the *bête noire* of most international mountaineers.

Greul did not climb mountains as Stuermer did 'because they were there'. He climbed to conquer, to show to the decadent Western World the strength, the power, the invinciblity of the new youthful National Socialist Germany. From that day in 1931 when he had conquered the North Face of the Eiger in winter as an 18-year old Hitler Youth Leader and shocked the Swiss by planting the hated Nazi flag on its summit, Gottfried Greul had regarded climbing as a political act : the conquest of each new mountain as a symbol of the strength of the new creed.

All the same, Stuermer told himself, the Major was one of the world's finest climbers and a brave soldier, who had served with Stormtroop Edelweiss right from the start. From Narvik in '40 to the Caucasian Passes last year, Major Greul had been in the forefront of the action, gaining the Knight's Cross of the Iron Cross, which presently bounced up and down around his throat, being wounded no less than six times in the process. He was a man to be reckoned with.

But then they all were in his elite little company. Every one of his men was hand-picked. All of them were pre-war professional climbers, tested in the Alps or Himalayas, or Bavarian or Austrian mountain boys who had learned to climb and ski before they could walk. Of course, they were

*The rare mountain flower, which Bavarian and Austrian boys risk their neck for in the heights, to give to their girlfriends as a sign of their love.

all individualists, lonely men, happy only when they were lost in the solitude and splendour of the mountains, who did not take kindly to discipline. But three years of war had taught them a kind of discipline – not that of the vast field-grey amorphous mass of the *Wehrmacht*, but that of the elite, each one of whom knew that he must submit to the will of the whole if Stormtroop Edelweiss was to succeed in the daring tasks which General Dietl, the Commander of the *Alpentruppen*, was constantly demanding of it.

Now they were climbing the saddle of the *Jungfraujoch*, which reminded Stuermer of the pictures of the one on Everest that the great English mountaineer, Mallory, had sent him just before his death on the unconquered mountain in 1924. Naturally it wasn't as tough as the one on the North Col of the Himalayan mountain, yet for the men of Stormtroop Edelweiss, who had done no serious climbing since their withdrawal from the Caucasus in the spring of 1943, it was a tough assignment. With a sudden grin on his bronzed, handsome face, Colonel Stuermer looked down at his men's sweat-lathered, strained features and told himself the climb would sweat all the good Bavarian beer out of their systems which they had imbibed ever since they had returned to the *Hochalpenkorps*' depot at Kufstein.

It was a thought which had occurred to 'Ox-Jo' Meier, Stormtroop Edelweiss's senior NCO too, as he clambered upwards, a forty-kilo mortar barrel strapped across his enormous back, his sweat-darkened tunic apparently about to split apart from the pressure of his straining shoulder muscles. Crimson-faced with effort, he turned his big cropped head and called down to his crony, Corporal Madad : 'Hey, Jap, what did you put in that shitty beer last night? Down-boy drops ! I feel like something scraped up from the bottom of a birdcage.'

'Jap' Madad, the issue of a passing relationship between the daughter of a Bavarian technician on the German-American reconnaissance of Nanga Parbat in 1920 and an amorous Hunza guide-porter, grinned. 'Yes, and you look it too, Ox,' he replied in perfect Bavarian, in spite of his exotic, un-German features which had given him his nickname in Stormtroop Edelweiss. 'But it isn't the beer, you know, Ox.'

'What is it, then?' Sergeant-Major Meier gasped.

'Five against one, that's what it is. Every time you do it, you lose ten precious drops of fluid from your spine, you know.' For a moment he freed one hand and with an explicit gesture he made it quite clear what he meant by five against one!

'What piggery!' the man above him snorted in mock disgust. 'That sort of thing might be all right for you lower rankers. But we senior noncoms have better things to do with it than waste it on the old five-fingered widow.'

'Will you NCOs stop that obscene babble down there at once.' It was Major Greul's incisive voice. 'Is your intellectual horizon limited only to theme number one?' he snapped angrily, his breath fogging around his arrogant face.

'Sorry sir,' Ox-Jo replied easily. 'Won't happen again, sir.'

The Major pulled at his waist karabiner.* 'Now come on. We've only got an hour to reach the peak before sunset.' He turned and concentrated on the business of climbing again.

Jawohl, Herr Major!' Ox-Jo said dutifully and when Greul's back was turned, stuck up the middle finger of his enormous gloved hand. 'Try that one on for size,' he muttered under his breath and winked at a grinning Jap.

The climb to the distant peak continued.

But the men of Stormtroop Edelweiss were not destined to reach the peak of the *Jungfraujoch* that particular September day. Just as the dying sun coloured the snowfield a blood-red, Colonel Stuermer in the lead was startled by a

---

*A snap-link on the climber's waist to which the climbing rope is attached.

sudden and peculiar sound – sharp, continuous and frightening.

He glanced upwards at the peak, already aware of what that dreaded sound implied; it was the same sound that had signified the end of the '37 Aiguilles de Chamonix Expedition which he had led. Above him the snow was beginning to crumble. White flurries spurted into the crystal clear air like a sudden fog. *'Lawine!'* he yelled urgently, fumbling for his climbing knife.

'Avalanche!' Major Greul took up the cry, reacting immediately like the professional he was, dropping his *alpenstock* and grabbing for his knife too. But already it was too late. With a monstrous roar the avalanche swept over the head of the long column of climbers, swamping them in its blinding snow-whirl. Ox-Jo, the last of the leading group, just had time to slash through the rope attaching him to the man behind him and then he too was submerged under the icy, choking mass.

Around Colonel Stuermer everything was blotted out by the flying white fog and for one appalling moment he thought he was going to be swept to his death. But he fought for control as the avalanche cascaded down the mountainside sweeping him, Greul and the two leading NCOs with it. He contrived somehow or other to prevent himself from being thrown backwards or onto his face, which could well have meant his death. Instead, enveloped by the snow and plunging downwards all the time, he managed to work himself away from the fast-moving centre of the snow channel, using his hands and legs as if he were swimming.

Gasping and spluttering for breath, feeling the weight of snow building up on top of his body, he sensed that the avalanche was ending. He exerted all his strength. He must not let himself be buried too deeply beneath the snow. Battling crazily, his arms and legs jerking like those of a puppet gone mad, he fought for space in the choking white mass.

To his surprise, he discovered that as the avalanche came

17

to a halt, his arms and legs were almost free. He crawled his way to the surface. Icy cold mountain air struck him across his burning face. He sucked in a great lungful gratefully. With a last heave, he pulled himself out of the clinging mass. It sighed like a reluctant lover and allowed him to go free. Then he was squatting on the confused surface of the snow, gasping like a runner after some tremendous race, concentrating solely on breathing in hugh gasps of the icy air.

'Herr Oberst!' the disembodied voice seemed to come from a long, long way off.

Reluctantly he raised his head. Far above him, silhouetted black against the blood-red ball of the setting sun, tiny figures were peering down at him. He performed a quick check. Most of the Company seemed to have survived the avalanche. But where were Greul, Madad, and above all, that big Bavarian rogue, 'Ox-Jo', the backbone of Stormtroop Edelweiss?

Hastily he rose to his feet and surveyed the scene, while the rest of the Company hurried down the mountainside. Fervently Stuermer prayed that the missing men had survived the two hundred metre drop.

A hand broke the surface of the snow. It wore a grey, chamois-leather glove. It could be only that of Greul, who affected such handwear instead of the *Wehrmacht* issue the rest of the Company wore. Stuermer stamped clumsily through the snow, and grasping the hand, tugged hard.

Greul's face broke through the surface of the snow, his mouth wide open and gaping, like that of a dying fish, as he sucked in the blessed air. Hastily Stuermer bent down. 'Are you all right, Greul?' he cried.

'Yes . . . yes,' the Major gasped. 'The . . . the others,. see . . . to the others.' While Greul sagged at the edge of the hole he had made for himself, Stuermer plodded across the surface of the snow, looking for the tell-tale signs of another hidden body.

He found Madad just as the rest of the Company came sliding down the mountainside to the scene of the accident.

18

He was conscious, but terribly chilled, his wizened Oriental face blanched and pinched with the cold, the icicles already beginning to form in his nostrils and eyebrows. All the same he had the strength to ask 'Where's Ox-Jo?' He grinned weakly with an effort. 'The big oaf still owes me ten Reichsmark from last payday.'

It was forty minutes before they found the missing Sergeant-Major. They discovered the spot where he was buried by the length of rope on the surface which he had cut in two to save the rest of the Company from being dragged over the edge of the saddle. But it was slow work loosening the snow and shovelling it away with their hands. All the same Ox-Jo was still conscious when they finally cleared the snow from him and found him wedged in a crevasse created by the mortar barrel tied to his back. Neither the fall, nor the suffocation, seemed to have done the Sergeant-Major any harm. His first words to the grinning troopers were : 'All right, knock the smiles off those ugly snouts of yours and get me out of here ! Or do you need a bloody written invitation to do so?'

Colonel Stuermer gave a smile of relief. Sergeant-Major Meier would live to fight another day.

Thus it was that the radio message reached Colonel Stuermer on the slope of the *Jungfraujoch* as he camped there for the night with his exhausted troopers. Holding the flimsy piece of paper that the radio operator had just handed him to the tiny hissing flames of the spirit cooker, Stuermer read the message aloud in a soft voice, the wind which swept across the snowfield almost drowning his words. 'Colonel Stuermer and Major Greul to report to General Dietl's Headquarters . . . zero eight hundred hours tomorrow morning . . . Walking-out uniform to be worn . . . Proceed Obersalzberg zero nine hundred hours . . . Dietl.'

He tendered the message to Greul, whose eyes shone excitedly in the reflected light of the little stove. He seized it eagerly and read it, while Stuermer stared thoughtfully at the velvet infinity of the night sky outside the tent.

'Obersalzberg, Colonel,' Greul cried. 'You know what that means, sir?'

Stuermer nodded, but said nothing, his eyes fixed almost sadly on the remote silver of the cold, unfeeling stars.

'We are to meet the *Führer*!'

'Yes, Greul. The *Führer* must be back from the East.'

'But what does it mean, sir?' Greul asked urgently. 'I mean General Dietl is to accompany us too.'

Stuermer did not answer immediately. He looked around the circle of little tents, his men silhouetted black against the golden light of the cooking stoves, and then beyond to the purity and sublimity of the mountain. Then he sighed and said in a voice full of the weariness of four years of war, 'It means, Major, that the *Führer* has a new mission for Stormtroop Edelweiss . . .'

THREE

'*Berg Heil!*' General Dietl cried happily at the door to his office in Kufstein's *Adolf Hitler Kaserne*, the HQ of the Fifth Mountain Corps.

'*Berg Heil, Herr General!*' the two officers returned the old mountaineer's greeting, snapping to attention.

Dietl nodded to Greul and extended his hand. 'How are you, Stuermer?'

'Very well, sir, thank you, except for a new collection of assorted bruises and abrasions I picked up yesterday.'

Dietl chuckled and motioned them to take a seat. 'You're getting too old for all that high alpine work of yours. 'He took up the stone bottle, decorated prettily with blue alpine flowers, 'Enzian, gentlemen?'

'Thank you, General,' Stuermer said promptly, 'though never trust a superior when he offers you a drink.'

Greul refused with an arrogant look which indicated

what he thought of officers, especially of the Alpine Corps, who began drinking at eight o'clock in the morning.

The other two did not notice. They clinked the glasses and downed the fiery Austrian drink in one.

'Well, General,' Stuermer said, eyeing the Commander under whom he had first served in the old days of the 3rd Mountain Division back at Narvik in 1940, 'where's the fire?'

Dietl gave him a wry smile. 'Have you heard of a place called Leros, Stuermer?' He walked to the big map of the Mediterranean which now covered the one of Russia which normally decorated one wall of his office. 'Here in the Aegean, just off the Turkish coast, about 140 kilometres from our main base in the Dodecanese on the Island of Rhodes.'

'And?' Stuermer and Greul queried as one, leaning forward to scan the map.

'The Tommies took it last week. I have a feeling that the *Führer* is going to give us the job of taking it back from them.'

Greul's face lit up at the prospect of action, but Stuermer's darkened. 'Not another Crete?' he snapped hastily.

Dietl shook his head. 'Everyone knows that Student's* paras would never be able to tackle anything like that again. Hitler would never allow them to go in first again and be slaughtered as they were at Crete in '41. The word from higher quarters is that this time the Alpine Corps goes in first. Once they have established themselves, the paras will drop on the island at the same time as the seaborne landing goes in.'

'But what is so damned important about Leros that the *Führer* is planning a full-scale landing on it, General?' Stuermer protested. 'I bet only one in ten Germans has ever heard of it.'

Dietl reached for his grey dress gloves. 'I don't know, Colonel. Perhaps we should leave the elucidation of that particular problem to the Greatest Captain of All Time,

*General Student, head of the German Parachute Corps.

our *Führer*, Adolf Hitler.' There was just a shadow of a smile on his face as he said these words.

They had driven across the old Austro-German frontier without difficulty, motored swiftly through the Ostertal in the remote Bavarian Alps and passed with painful slowness through one well-guarded barrier after another until finally, with only minutes to spare, they had been escorted by one of the SS officers adjutants, who dwarfed even Greul, into the ante-room at Obersalzberg. Black-clad, immaculate aides sped back and forth. Generals and admirals, important looking folders under their arms, popped in and out of the door. Once Bormann, the 'Brown Eminence' himself, poked his bullet-head through the door to check who was still in the ante-room.

'Flap,' Dietl hissed out of the side of his mouth.

'You're right, General,' Stuermer agreed. In these last terrible years he had seen it all before : the hectic activity, which would end tamely enough for the high officers concerned but which would mean destruction and sudden death for many a weary, stubblehopper on some faraway front. 'But why?'

But before General Dietl could answer that question, the great twin doors were flung open by an immensely tall SS adjutant. Eyes fixed on some distant horizon like some stage butler, he said tonelessly : *'Meine Herren, der Führer lässt bitten!'* Hurriedly the three officers grabbed their soft peaked caps, thrust them under their right arms at the regulation angle, and strode smartly into the huge room, dominated by the mighty picture window that offered a spectacular view of the Untersberg, Berchtesgaden and Salzburg. Adolf Hitler, the master of all of Europe from the Channel Coast to the Caucasus, spun round and faced the three Alpine Corps officers. For a moment he stared at them blankly; then he smiled revealing a row of yellow teeth and said, 'Ah, my dear General Dietl, good of you to come.'

He looked at Stuermer, the tall bronzed mountaineer,

and was obviously pleased with what he saw. He stretched out both his hands and took Stuermer's broad hand in them 'The conqueror of Mount Elbrus,' he exclaimed. 'It is an honour to meet you, Colonel'*

If Stuermer had not been so deeply tanned, his blush at the effusive praise, which was so typical of the National Socialist *prominenz* and which he so heartily detested, would have been visible. *'Jawohl, mein Führer,'* was all that he managed to stammer. 'Thank you.'

Hitler smiled and slapped him on the shoulder heartily and chortled. 'Well now, my dear Colonel, I am going to give your unit a chance to emulate and perhaps even outdo that tremendous coup of yours. Follow me, gentlemen.' Obediently the three officers trailed after him to the great window and stood there in expectant silence while Hitler stared at the tremendous mountain view. 'Gentlemen,' he announced suddenly, using that oblique approach of his which always caught his visitors off guard, 'Legend has it that Emperor Charlemagne sleeps out there in the Untersberg, waiting for the day when he must rise once more and restore the German Empire. It is no accident that I, Adolf Hitler, have made my home opposite it. It is a continual inspiration to me that even at the moment of deepest crisis, a great man can rise again and master a seemingly hopeless situation.' Suddenly he swung round on them, his face sombre, but his dark eyes blazing fanatically. 'And at this very moment we Germans are involved in a grave crisis, a very grave one indeed.'

He strode to the huge table and pressed a button. The wall covering slid back to reveal an enormous map of the Mediterranean.

'I have been betrayed in Italy,' he snapped. 'Already the enemy is landing troops there with the connivance of that pack of traitors around their King.'

'So now that drunken sot, Churchill, thinks he can use

*The highest peak in the Caucasus and the furthest penetration into Southern Russia achieved by German troops, conquered by Stormtroop Edelweiss in the third week of August, 1942.

Italy's collapse to roll up our whole southern flank. I can read his addled mind like a book. First he will take the Dodecanese – the landings at Leros and Kos are only a prelude to the capture of Rhodes, the key to the whole Aegean. Once he has the island group, then he will attack our communications in Greece, reinforce that Red terrorist Tito. The bombing of the Rumanian oilfields will follow and the supply of Russia via the Dardanelles instead of the Artic and Persian Gulf routes. But above all gentlemen, Churchill will use the possession of the Dodecanese and the Aegean to force the Turks into the war on the Allied side. And you know what that will mean?'

'That we will be forced to abandon Southern Russia?' Dietl ventured.

'Not just *Southern* Russia; the whole of that accursed country,' Hitler snarled. 'If the Turks came in, we would be under the severest pressure there. But,' he raised his finger as if addressing the crowd at one of the pre-war Nuremberg Party Rallies, 'Turkey will not join the enemy, as long as we have Rhodes. From there we can bombard her south-western coast and bomb her most populous cities. Ankara would never stand that. Thus it is vital that Rhodes remains in our hands. You understand that, gentlemen? *Rhodes must stay German!*'

'*Jawohl, mein Führer!*' they answered as one, caught up by the tremendous magnetism of the man facing them.

'That is the reason why I have called you officers together,' Hitler continued, his voice calm again. 'Today you will be briefed by Colonel-General Jodl on the operation to prevent Rhodes from falling into the enemy's hands. Gentlemen, I shall dismiss you now for your briefing. But remember this. The whole future of the war and the fate of the Reich may well depend on what will happen on that remote little Greek island.' He stared at them with those dark hypnotic eyes of his, a note almost of pleading in his voice. '*Gentlemen, give me Leros!*'

FOUR

'Leros', the pale-faced General said, 'fifty kilometres by ten.' He smiled, but his light, cynical eyes did not grow any warmer. 'One could spit from one end of it to the other.'

The other three stared at Jodl's detailed map, noting the mountainous character of the island and realizing immediately why the Alpine Corps had been called in for this operation.

'Before the enemy invaded,' Jodl continued, 'it was garrisoned mainly by Italian troops under the command of an Admiral Mascherpa. There were 5,500 of them, mainly engaged in administrative work at the naval base at Leros and manning the twenty-four naval batteries, armed with one hundred guns of various types and calibres. In addition there was an infantry detachment of one thousand men, armed with out-of-date equipment. Most of the Italian troops were either reservists or from the older draft categories.' As always, Hitler's Chief-of-Staff reeled off the figures and details without any reference to notes; it was a characteristic that usually impressed his listeners. But it did not impress Colonel Stuermer. His gaze was still fixed on those mountains, his mind dominated by one overwhelming question : what would be the role of Stormtroop Edelweiss?

'Now as far as we can gather from aerial reconnaissance,' Jodl was saying, 'our former Allies have seen the error of their ways and have undergone an instant conversion to the freedom-loving, western democratic way of life.' He smiled at the three officers cynically. 'In other words, the Spaghettis have gone over to the enemy. At least, they don't seem to have put up any resistance to the invaders.'

'In what kind of strength did the enemy land, Colonel-General?' Dietl asked.

'They put ashore what appears to be a regiment of

infantry. Three thousand men, a brigade as the British call it. In their usual antiquated manner, their command has made one battalion responsible for one of the three geographical areas into which Leros can be split. A German commander would have concentrated his forces. By doing so, the British are playing into our hands. In essence, they have a thousand men in the north, another thousand in the centre and the final thousand in the south; each group is more or less self-contained. From the distribution of their forces, we can safely conclude that they intend to cover the whole of the coastal area against a seaborne invasion. This will mean—'

'Dissipation of their strength, leaving them wide-open for an airborne landing in the interior,' Dietl interrupted eagerly.

'Exactly, my dear Dietl,' Jodl said. 'Especially as Intelligence informs us that the roads on the island are few, narrow and bad, capable of taking nothing larger than one of the enemy's jeeps.

'As you rightly conclude, Dietl,' he continued, 'we will therefore make an airborne landing to the enemy's rear at the narrow neck of land between Gurna and Alinda Bays, with the aim of cutting off the northern and central forces of the enemy. At the same time as the airborne landing is taking place, our seaborne forces under General Mueller will land and attack from the north at Parteni Bay and from the south at Pandeli Bay.' He beamed at them. 'All very neat and tidy, you will probably say. An excellent piece of staff work and planning. But there is a fly in the ointment, gentlemen – the two heights which dominate the centre of the island – here at Mount Clidi, and here at Mount Meraviglia.'

Greul, his eyes glowing, flashed a significant look at Stuermer. The Colonel nodded his head in unspoken agreement; now they knew what Stormtroop Edelweiss's assignment in the coming invasion of Leros would be.

'Now both of those heights are fortified and possess

26

THE ISLAND OF LEROS,
SEPTEMBER-NOVEMBER, 1943

THE PLAN OF ATTACK

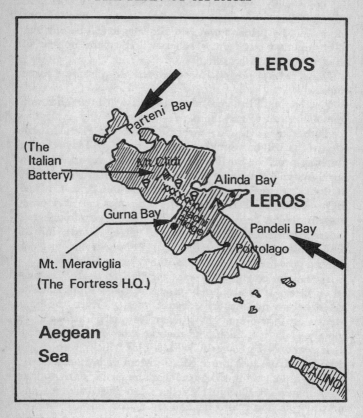

LEROS

Parteni Bay

(The Italian Battery)

Mt. Chu?

Alinda Bay

LEROS

Gurna Bay

Pandeli Bay

Portolago

Mt. Meraviglia
(The Fortress H.Q.)

Aegean Sea

CALINO

→ The seaborne attack

♉ The airborne attack

artillery, which according to Admiral Canaris'* spies among the local population covers the coast. Being Greek, the spies are amenable to persuasion.' Jodl made a gesture of counting coins with his finger and thumb. 'They report that Mount Clidi is manned by Italian artillery and Mount Meraviglia by British gunners. Naturally it will be our task to ensure that our former Allies will have the honour of crossing swords with us first.'

'*Das Hochalpenkorps, Herr General?*' Major Greul asked eagerly.

'Yes, Major. First you mountaineers will take Clidi and immobilize the guns there. They present the most immediate danger to our airborne landing. Then Mount Meraviglia will be your objective. Not only will it present a climbing problem, but I'm sure your Bavarian and Austrian farmboys will overcome that one—' Dietl frowned severely at Jodl's arrogant sarcasm. 'It also is the British Island HQ – Fortress Headquarters the Tommies call it. Consequently it will be defended to the last. A very tough nut indeed, gentlemen.' He paused and let his words sink in, while Stuermer stared at the map already trying to work out the best line of ascent from the contour-lines.

'Now, gentlemen,' Jodl went on, 'let me make this perfectly clear. It is absolutely essential that Mount Clidi is taken before the airborne assault goes in. Even the Spaghettis are brave enough to massacre our paratroopers in the air. Once it is taken and the paratroopers have landed, your rear will be covered. With a bit of luck, even if you do not manage to capture Mount Meraviglia immediately, you might be able to shake the Tommies sufficiently to take their minds off General Mueller's landings to south and north. Well, that is all I have to say. *Questions?*'

Stuermer spoke for the first time since they had entered the makeshift operations room. 'General, you said we would go in *before* the airborne assault. What is the date of the operation and how do we go in?'

Jodl looked at him keenly and obviously liked what he

*Head of the *Abwehr*, the German Intelligence Service.

28

saw. Perhaps Stuermer's clipped, educated North German accent, so different from Dietl's thick coarse Bavarian, told him that he was dealing with one of his own kind. 'The operation will begin on the night of 11 November, with General Mueller's landings and the paradrop scheduled to take place at zero four hundred hours on the morning of the twelfth. Your mountaineers, Stuermer, must be in position on Leros by dawn on the eleventh.'

Stuermer started. 'That means we shall be on the island a full twenty-four hours before the invasion actually starts!'

'Exactly, my dear Colonel,' Jodl agreed smoothly. 'Now *how* you go in,' he continued, 'is rather more complicated. We must ensure absolute secrecy otherwise the British will start building up their defences at Leros, instead of concentrating on their proposed attack on Rhodes. Therefore your mountaineers will proceed to Leros like this . . .'

When he had finished his explanation of how Stormtroop Edelweiss would be smuggled out of Germany to Kattavia on Rhodes whence they would start the operation against Leros, Stuermer began to smile. 'General, I doubt if my men are going to enjoy the experience, but if I may say so, it is an ingenious plan.'

Jodl nodded his appreciation. 'Thank you for saying so, Colonel, but remember this. The enemy will have his eyes everywhere along the route you take. Once he realizes that the boats are carrying mountain troops, it won't take him long to guess where you're heading. You must take every precaution to ensure that that eventuality does not arise. For if the enemy does discover your objective, Stormtroop Edelweiss will be walking straight into a trap . . .'

FIVE

'Fit you call yourselves!' Major Greul sneered at them contemptuously, hands on hips, his muscular legs astride, hardly breathing hard in spite of what they had just been through.

'Fit to drop!' Ox-Jo muttered under his breath, trying to control his wildly heaving chest.

'Where have you been training? In the local drinking halls and brothels no doubt! In all my time in the High Alpine Corps, I don't think I've ever seen such a bunch of weak-kneed, soft-gutted men as you this morning.' His hard eyes swept along the line of crimson-faced men, who had just completed the Company's battle course. 'But I'm going to teach you that our Folk Comrades back in the Reich are not paying a bunch of layabouts a decent wage so that you can drink beer and fornicate the days away. No sir!'

'Fornicate,' Meier told himself weakly. 'I've not got the strength to fuck a fly!'

'Sergeant-Major,' Greul barked, turning on the big NCO. 'Sir?'

'Another five kilos per man,' he ordered.

Meier thought better of protesting. Turning round he faced the exhausted mountain troopers. 'All right, come on, get the lead out of your arses! The Major hasn't got all day!'

Wearily, each trooper opened his rucksack, which already weighed forty-five kilos and added another 20mm shell from the pile at the bottom of the rock face.

Greul placed his whistle to his lips and shrilled three blasts on it.

The Company streamed forward at the double. '*Tempo . . . tempo!*' the Major cried, running at their side like a sheep dog harrying a flock.

The first group reached the line of ropes hanging down from the metal pitons hammered into the rock face fifty metres above their heads. As one, they grabbed them and began to climb upwards, the rucksacks tearing at their muscles. Major Greul disdained the use of a rope. He clambered up the rock face at an impossible speed, finding hand and footholds that another climber would not even have seen.

The first group flung themselves over the top, black spots leaping in wild patterns in front of their eyes, blood pounding furiously in their ears. But there was to be no rest for them yet.

'Attack formation;' Greul barked.

The troopers unslung their rifles. To both flanks, Spandaus opened up. A criss-cross of white tracer zipped alarmingly across their front some fifty metres away, moving forward with them, as they struggled up the steep grassy slope. 'Keep up . . . keep up !' Greul yelled, excited as always by gunfire.

They reached the spur of rock, standing upright from the slope. It was the spot. From higher up hosepipes had begun to gush water, turning the last half of the slope into a sea of mud.

Greul gave them no chance to rest. *'Hinlegen!'* he commanded above the savage hiss of the Spandaus.

Before them lay twenty metres of mud, above which rose a maze of barbed wire, skewered to the ground with just enough room for a soldier to wriggle under if he kept his body low.

'Forward !'

Rifles balanced across their arms, weighed down by that tremendous load, they began to crawl forward, arms and legs jerking awkwardly like the wooden joints of puppets. The mud was as slippery as ice. The wire ripped at their flesh and clothing. Rucksacks stuck and while the angry white tracer winged above their bare heads, the gasping troopers fought to free themselves.

Their ordeal was not over yet. Gasping and choking, they struggled to their feet. One hundred metres away a set of wooden targets had been set up. 'When I give the order, open fire,' Greul ordered. 'And woe betide anyone who fails to get one bull. *FIRE AT WILL!*'

With trembling hands, they raised their rifles and tried

to focus on the weaving blur of the targets. The ragged volley rang out all along the mountainside.

Greul could hardly wait for them to finish the five-round fire pattern. He bounded forward, carrying the 50 kilo rucksack on his broad shoulders as if it contained feathers not shells. Lightly the Major ran from target, shouting in disgust as he noted the absence of bulls on each target.

Eventually he swung round, his eyes blazing with contempt and anger. 'Great God,' he barked, 'what is wrong with you men? No bull on every second target. By Christ, I'll teach you bunch of weak mothers to shoot, if it's the last thing I do. I swear it in the name of the *Führer*! Sergeant-Major, take them through it again!'

Like dying men, their eyes devoid of any emotion but absolute exhaustion, they staggered down the slope to begin the course again.

'Train hard, fight easy,' Greul repeated his favourite maxim. Colonel Stuermer sniffed and stared at the men lined up ready for the night exercise. 'You mustn't overdo it, Greul,' he warned. 'You can work a man too hard, you know.'

'Beg permission to disagree, sir,' Greul said. 'You can't make an omelette without cracking eggs.'

Stuermer ran his eyes along the lines of waiting men. In a way he had to agree. The troopers of Stormtroop Edelweiss had never looked fitter. Under Greul's harsh regime, the men had lost all superfluous flesh. Their bodies were spare and lean, their eyes luminous, faces tanned. 'All right, Greul, you can take them away. But no more broken limbs please. We're going to need every man soon.'

Major Greul could not refrain from sneering. 'Let us weed out the weak in heart and body now. Only the hard and the brave deserve the honour of shedding their blood for the Fatherland.'

'Oh, get on with it, Greul,' Stuermer said a little wearily. Yet moments later when Stormtroop Edelweiss marched out of the barracks with a confident swing, he felt a sudden glow of pride in his men.

32

'Schwarzbraun muss mein Madel sein
Genauso wie ich . . .
Hei -di, hei -do, hei -ja . . .'

As the marching song echoed and re-echoed down the stone chasm of the *Hermann Goeringstrasse*, wooden shutters were flung open everywhere and curious faces peered out at the marching men below.

At the end of the column Sergeant-Major Meier, marching next to Jap, looked up and saw her for the first time. She leaned over the carved wooden balcony, the cleavage formed by her magnificent breasts in the low cut dress looking like the valley of the *Jungfraujoch* itself.

Meier faltered and almost lost the step. *'Jesus, Maria, Joseph!'* he breathed in sheer awe. He growled low in his throat, as the big blonde with the tremendous breasts bent even lower over her window boxes, to wave excitedly at the departing soldiers. 'Oh brother, I'd give a month's pay to get my poor old head in between those beauties!' 'Big-Lunged Laura,' Jap informed him as they swung into the *Adolf Hitler Platz*, 'wife of SA Leader Lorenz.'

'You mean that a civilian, even if he is a SA man, is allowed to put his miserable dick into that delightful creature?' Meier asked increduously between snatches of the chorus. 'If the *Führer* only knew!'

As they started the long ascent into the mountains for the night exercise, and their singing died away, a plan began to form in Sergeant-Major Meier's head.

'Tonight we practise the Tryolean,' Greul announced, as they stood facing the Major. 'You've all used the technique before on the high summits. Tonight we are going to assume that we are on a seacliff face and that we need the device to cross a seacave.'

Meier looked at Jap significantly and whispered out of the side of his mouth. 'So that's it? We're in for a little sea trip, if I'm not mistaken.'

All that night they practised the Tryolean in groups of

33

five. Ascending an adjacent peak, they would lasso the summit they intended to climb and having secured their ropes, slide across in a highly dangerous and wildly exciting manoeuvre. Time and time again Greul would bellow at some unfortunate sailing through the night air across the void to the opposite rock wall : 'Pull up your damned feet, man ! That's the sea down below you there. *UP WITH THOSE FEET!*'

Just as the first dirty-white light of the false dawn began to flush the mountain sky, he cried : 'All right, that's the end of the Tyrolean exercise !'

There were sighs of relief everywhere. All the men wanted now was to get back to their Kufstein barracks and flop into their bunks. But that was not to be. The next moment, the Major announced, 'Now, so that we finish off the exercise properly, we're going to run down the mountain. It will teach you to pick up your big feet.' He drew his pistol. 'And just to ensure that we really stretch our legs and run, I'll be behind you with this.' His voice rose. 'About turn !'

The mountain troopers swung round and stared down at the valley far below, the town of Kufstein, still wreathed in shadows, in its centre.

'All right, now. *RUN!*'

In a shower of dust and stones, they descended the sixty degree slope of the cliff face. Some slid down on their backsides, their field-grey trousers ripped to shreds in an instant. Others banged and bounced from one boulder to another, their hands bruised and dripping with blood. Meier, screaming with maniacal glee, zoomed down from bush to bush, feeling his arms almost ripped from their sockets as they gripped each new hold.

Finally, choking, moaning, purple in the faces, blood pouring from a myriad cuts, they crashed into the first pines of the tree line and came to a stop at last.

'*Ach, du lieber Zeit!*' Colonel Stuermer exclaimed as he looked at the men of Stormtroop Edelweiss, lined up on the morning square in front of him for inspection. 'What a sorry bunch they are!

'What did you do with them, Greul?' he enquired, hardly believing the evidence of his own eyes.

'We did a mountain run, Colonel.'

'*At night?*'

'Yes sir.'

'Then they must have reached an excellent state of training if they can come down the mountains in darkness like that, Greul. My congratulations, Major,' Colonel Stuermer added in grudging admiration.

'There is always room for further improvement. The Tryolean went—'

'But I'm afraid, there isn't,' Stuermer interrupted the Major. 'I received a blitz* from the *Führer*'s HQ half an hour ago. We move out in forty-eight hours. We'll have the Company Booze-Up tonight. Training is over for Stormtroop Edelweiss. The fun and games can begin once more!'

SIX

'Enough, enough, the maiden cried, I'm satisfied,' Sergeant-Major Meier said to no one in particular. He pushed away his plate which was littered with a small mountain of well-picked bones. He was in high good humour this evening. Even the prespect of active service did not worry him. He had eaten his fill of *eisbein und sauerkraut*, there was free beer and schnaps paid for by the officers, and at the back of his mind, there was the thought of Big-Lunged Laura.

'You know why we're here.' Meier bawled. 'This is Stormtroop Edelweiss's last company booze-up before we move out. So before you lot of hairy-arsed mountain-climbers get bombed out of your Bavarian minds, I want you to listen to the Colonel.'

Major Greul, toying with his mug of beer, frowned. He did not like these company evenings when the men ate

*An Express telegram.

and drank too much. He knew they were a German Army tradition, but the overindulgence offended his sense of National Socialist frugality and single-minded dedication. At his side, Colonel Stuermer grinned. It was typical Meier, he told himself. He had had his fill now he was eager to get on with the serious part of the evening – beer swilling.

Stuermer looked round their faces, bronzed, lean and hard, and liked what he saw. With the exception of a few replacements like Lieutenant Sepplmayr sitting opposite him, the troopers were all veterans who had been with him from the start of the war. They were probably the best mountain troops in the world. Yet their new assignment was going to be difficult and dangerous.

'*Comrades!* You all know the purpose of this evening? Soon we shall be leaving Kufstein. I am afraid I cannot give you details, but our mission, which is a vital one for the success of German arms, is not without danger.

'But I know I can rely on each and every one of you.' Stuermer's gaze swept their serious faces. 'Just as you can rely upon me. I will not ask you to do anything I cannot do myself. I shall expect the utmost from you, but I will do all that is in my power to ensure casualties are kept low.'

Next to the standing Colonel, Greul sneered. Had not the *Führer* himself said that when 'blood flowed, it purified'? A German should not be afraid of dying for his Folk, Fatherland and *Führer*.

Stuermer ignored the look on his second-in-command's face. Instead he raised his beer mug and cried : '*Long live Stormtroop Edelweiss!*'

The Company sprang to their feet as one. Their heavy, nailed mountain boots crashed down on the scrubbed wooden floor as they came to the position of attention, litre mugs of beer level with the third button of their tunics as military custom prescribed.

'*Long Live Stormtroop Edelweiss!*' they roared back.

'*EX!*' Stuermer commanded.

'No heel-taps,' they echoed his order.

The men raised their mugs to their lips, drained them

36

and slapped the mugs down on the trestle table with all their might, as if they wished to smash through the thick oak. The Company Booze-Up could begin.

'Did you hear the one about the hausfrau who was sick of rationing?' Jap yelled excitedly above the roar, 'who asked the butcher if he had any blood sausage. No, he said, he hadn't any blood sausage. Well, do you have any liver sausage, she asks. No, he ain't got any liver sausage, he says. Well have you got tongue, she asks. Yes tongue I've got, he says. *Then lick my arse with it*, she shouts and takes off . . .'

Colonel Stuermer smiled. How many times had he sat in such smoke-filled rooms, heavy with the fumes of beer and cigars, listening to the same old drunken jokes in these last few years. Somewhere the omnipotent, impersonal generals sitting in their remote headquarters were poring over the same maps of the same terrain, preparing to match their moral strength and their tactical ingenuity against one another in a kind of lethal chess game. And it would be these men, honest, simple soldiers, and the millions like them in all the world's armies, who would be the victims of those generals and their tactics.

Suddenly Colonel Stuermer had had enough of the company booze-up. He picked up his cap, with the metal Edelweiss badge, from the table already dripping with spilled beer and rose to his feet.

Meier saw him do so out of the corner of his eye. He was about to jump up and call the room to attention. Silently Stuermer shook his head and indicated that the men should not be disturbed; they should be allowed to continue drinking. Touching his hand to the peak of his mountain cap, as if in salute to these young men who were going to be sacrificed, he slipped quietly into the cold night.

Ox-Jo drank steadily, but carefully, a thoughtful frown on his face. The Company was pretty drunk. Lieutenant Sepplmayr, their newest officer and as accident-prone as ever, had been sick down the front of his tunic. Major Greul had swept out, dragging an unhappy, deathly pale Sepplmayr with him. Everywhere the smoke-filled room was littered with 'beer corpses', drunken mountain-troopers sprawled over the soaked tables.

Meier's mind was full of Laura, that magnificent Austrian Laura with those monstrous white breasts that seemed about to explode out of her embroidered bodice every time she took a deep breath. He could just imagine taking one of them in each of his hands and rubbing the nipples together as if they were kissing. Then he'd flip them up and down, as if he were juggling, watching the pretty pink nipples shivering excitedly. After that he'd get her to press them together, forming a valley and taking a bottle of champagne he'd . . .

He clicked off his private blue film projector, his decision made. He was going to be up Big-Lunged Laura's knickers that night, or his name wasn't Ox-Jo Meier !

The black-out outside was perfect. Not a light showed anywhere, and the sky above his head was empty of stars. For a moment he stood swaying there, trying to orientate himself, realizing as the cold night air struck him in the face that he had drunk more than he had thought.

Hands held in front of him like a blind man, he groped his way to the shed. His boot thudded against the door. It flew open. 'Now where's the ladder?' he muttered to himself and laughed drunkenly.

He found the ladder and wrenched it from the hooks. With a grunt he swung it over his shoulder and began to head drunkenly for the exit to the barracks. 'Do you love me, darling, she'll say,' he crooned to himself, 'or is that just a revolver in your pocket?'

Swaying alarmingly, Jap stood next to the wall and watched him pass, hardly believing what his eyes told him he was seeing. Sergeant-Major Meier going off to indulge in a little bit of old-fashioned fornication ! Suddenly he made up his mind too. 'Hey, hang on, Ox,' he cried, 'I'm coming with you !'

38

SEVEN

'Drunk last night . . . drunk the night before . . . gonna get drunk tonight like I've never been drunk before . . .
Bawling the song at the top of his voice, Ox-Jo had just staggered out of the *Adolf Hitler Platz* into the *Herman Goeringstrasse,* where the celebrated Laura lived, when a flashlight flicked on and blinded him.

'And just where do you think you're off to with that ladder, Sergeant-Major?' a hard voice demanded.

Meier staggered to a surprised stop in front of the two menacing figures. 'I've just fallen out of my bed. I need the ladder to fucking well get in again, you Prussian prick.'

The man who had spoken in the harsh North German voice pressed his torch against his chest and Ox-Jo caught a glimpse of a helmeted, square-jawed face above the silver crescent plate of the military police around his neck.

'Christ!' he exclaimed, *'Headhunters!'*

'Yes, we're from the Field Gendarmerie,' the voice agreed. 'Now where are you going with that ladder?'

'Take off, chaindog,' Ox-Jo said, 'or there'll be a carve-up here.'

'Sergeant-Major, I can shit on you,' the headhunter said threateningly, 'from a great height.' Something cold and metallic clicked round Meier's right wrist.

But before he could attach the other handcuff, a thing like an ancient monkey dropped on his back.

'Jap!' Meier gasped.

'Well, don't stand there like a fart in a trance,' the little half-breed cried 'plant one on the other shit!'

Like a steam shovel Meier's fist hit the bigger of two MPs and sent him flying through the darkness. Meier lashed out again. The other MP groaned once and dropped to the pavement without another sound. 'He'll need a new

39

set of choppers tomorrow morning, if I'm not mistaken,' Meier said smugly.

'Pick up the ladder, Ox!' Jap urged, as the night stillness was broken by the shrilling of police whistles. A moment later the two of them were running wildly for Big-Lunged Laura's window.

Meier shook his head. The bedroom came into focus, but his vision was still blurred. Slowly he turned his head round. Clothes were everywhere. A beer-stained tunic, for some reason two pairs of mountain boots, his underpants screwed into a ball, a woman's sweater spreadeagled over the chair.

He swung his head to look at the enormous bulk of woman lying next to him in the big bed. Through sticky eyes, he caught sight of those tremendous twin mountains of flesh surmounted by their rosy summits, rising and falling steadily.

Meier licked his lips and said : 'Just a quickie, Laura, for old times' sake.' He smiled slowly and reached out an experimental finger and thumb to pinch the nearest nipple.

But before he could do so a dirty hand swept over from the other side of the big bed and playfully tweaked Laura's other nipple.

He sat up and stared across Laura, who had her eyes tightly closed, her breath coming more quickly now, a little smile of secret pleasure on her big white face. A naked figure lay there, huddled with his head next to Laura's breast like a child. *'JAP,'* he exploded. *'YOU!'*

The little corporal opened his eyes. 'Who did you expect – the *Führer*?' Laura sat up, her face set in a tired but happy look. 'Now my little cheetahs,' she breathed warningly. 'We all had a good time, didn't we?' She looked from one soldier to the other. 'At least, I did.'

Ox-Jo slapped his big paw against his forehead melodramatically, 'But you can't have all your cups in your cupboard to let . . . let that pygmy have you! I mean he's 'not even a proper Bavarian.' He bunched his fist and looked at Jap threateningly.

'Part of him is,' Laura said and looked at the little man huddled against her massive flanks lovingly.

'Haven't you got a sense of humour, Ox?' Jap parried. 'Smile and give yer ears a visit!' Big-Lunged Laura sat up between them; *'Meine Herren . . . meine Herren,'* she commanded, holding up her hands for peace. 'Why so much noise in the early morning? The day hasn't begun yet and we want to start it the proper way, don't we?'

Meier lowered his fist and looked at her suspiciously. 'What do you mean – the proper way?'

She giggled, the rolls of flesh across her stomach trembling as she did so. 'Well, what do you think I mean, Sergeant-Major Meier?' she sobbed, tears of pleasure trickling down her cheeks.

Ox-Jo's mouth flopped open like that of a stranded fish. 'You don't mean,' he gasped stupidly.

'Why not?' she answered, wiping her eyes.

'All right,' he said finally. 'But that half-breed pygmy has got to keep his eyes closed while I'm at it.'

'Who said you're getting firsters?' Jap protested.

'How are we gonna do it?' Meier interrupted.

'Heads or tails?' Laura suggested.

'You mean toss for it?'

She nodded her head, a modest smile of anticipation on her face.

But neither Jap nor Ox-Jo was fated to enjoy 'firsters' that morning. Just as Laura had steadied the ten pfennig coin on her thumb a familiar sound floated through the window against which the ladder was still propped.

'The reveille bugle at the barracks,' Jap cried. 'Isn't it the bloody end! Just when a bloke's about to get a bit of the other, too.'

Ox-Jo sprang naked from the bed and grabbed his boots. 'Come on, Jap,' he yelled 'haul ass. Edelweiss is off today and the Colonel'll have my balls off if I'm late.'

'And me? Laura asked in consternation, as the two men

flung themselves frantically into their uniforms, while from across the way came the sound of the barracks waking up for another day of war.

Jap grabbed the candle from the holder. 'Here,' he cried, 'take this.' He flung the candle into her naked lap. If Town Leader Lorenz can't do you any more good, that'll have to keep you happy till the lads of Stormtroop Edelweiss get back from the wars.' And with that the two of them were gone through the open window, laughing uproariously . . .

Part Two

A VOYAGE TO RHODES

ONE

'Shit;' Ox-Jo cursed, and staring gloomily at the slowly passing valley of the Moselle, he spat over the side of the boat.

'What's up, Ox?' Jap asked, amused at his companion's gloom.

Meier tugged at his short civilian jacket for the umpteenth time that day and said, 'Everything's up, you little slant-eyed half-cast. I thought we were in the Alpine Corps, not in the fucking Navy.' He waved a big hand at the other three boats following them down the river, their engines throbbing idly at five knots an hour.

Jap flipped his cigarette end over the side. 'What are you worried about? Nobody's trying to blow your stupid head off are they?'

'You know me – I get sea-sick just looking at the Isar*. Besides what's this lark about?'

'What lark?'

'These civvies and those bloody boats!' He nodded at the S-boats, disguised as tugs, their guns removed, their white hulls painted black and brown. 'Fake funnels and fake bridges made of wood. Where the hell are we off to, I ask you? It must be a mission.'

'But not in Frogland,' Jap protested, indicating France which lay ahead further up the river. 'We've had no trouble with the Frogs since forty.'

'Of course not, you stupid shit! The only action you'll see in Frogland is in some whore's bed, and the way we're going, there'll be no nooky for the lads of Edelweiss this trip.'

Meier's gloomy prognosis was right. Ever since Jodl had revealed his plan to Stuermer, the Commander of Stormtroop Edelweiss had insisted on total security. The Company

*A Bavarian river.

had moved from Kufstein at dead of night, had transferred to a fleet of civilian trucks on the *autobahn* east of Cologne just before dawn and had been ordered to change into the civilian clothes waiting for them in the trucks. That same night they had been smuggled aboard the camouflaged S-boats to transport them down the German-French river and canal system to the Ligurian Sea and from there across the Mediterranean to Rhodes. Now, as the S-boats chugged their way through Luxembourg towards the pre-war French frontier, Colonel Stuermer explained his plans for their trip through France to Greul and *Korvettenkapitan* Doerr, the commander of the S-boat group. 'You see,' he said, forced to crouch a little in the tiny, low-roofed cabin,' our security problems will really start once we enter France. There we must assume that everyone is against us and will have the means to pass on information to the Tommies' intelligence service.'

Doerr, a small burly officer with prematurely greying hair, nodded his agreement. 'Yes, you are right there, Colonel. Within twenty-four hours of our real purpose being detected that information will be in London.'

'Now according to your estimate, Doerr, it will take us three days to get down to the Mediterranean.'

'Yes, Colonel.'

'It is a devil of a long time, gentlemen, moving at this speed, subject to perusal from both banks and other vessels which we will encounter on our route.'

'I think Operation False Nose should fool most observers,' Doerr remarked. 'We have been using this disguise trick as a standard operating procedure to transfer boats from the Channel to the Med for two years now.' He grinned suddenly. 'We pinched it from the Tommies, who used it in '39 and '40 before we kicked their upper-class arses out of Europe for good.'

Stuermer grinned too. The easy-going, yet highly experienced naval officer was a pleasant person to get along with, especially after Greul's haughtiness. 'That may be so, Doerr. But you mustn't forget a normal tug doesn't carry as

46

many men as are now on board. I'm sure that any experienced riverman would realize that a tug of this size would not need the thirty-odd we've got to work it.'

'Agreed,' Doerr said promptly, his grin vanishing.

'So we must ensure that my troopers only go on deck in small numbers and preferably after dark . . . You will draw up a roster for each boat, Greul.

'Now, according to the *Abwehr*,' Stuermer continued, 'the real danger from spies will threaten once we have crossed the old demarcation line between Occupied and Vichy France on the Saône between Seurre and Chalon-sur-Saône. Before we marched into Vichy France last winter, the area apparently was full of Resistance spy groups. Since we moved in, the Gestapo and the *Abwehr* have done their best to round them up. But according to my informant, there are still plenty of them at large and reporting to London. It is my intention, therefore, to complete that last stage of our journey to the Mediterranean without stopping.'

Doerr tugged the end of his nose thoughtfully. 'We'll be moving from the Saône into the Rhône just after dark at our present speed,' he said slowly. 'If we raised our speed to ten knots we could reach the coast a couple of hours after dawn. Naturally at that speed and in the dark, we would run the risk of a collision with a barge or something. After all, this is the first time most of my officers have navigated this trip down the inland waterways.'

'That is a risk we must take,' Stuermer said sombrely.

'But what about the next twenty-four hours?' Greul said. He pointed through the little porthole at the white arrow on the concrete wall of the river bank and the legend *Sierck-les-Bains, 5 km*. 'Sierck's the French frontier. Won't there be spies there too?'

'The *Abwehr* says no, Greul. Lorraine has been in our hands since 1940. Much of the population is German-speaking and friendly to our cause. Those who were not have long passed behind Swedish curtains.' He stretched the fingers of his right hand in front of his face like prison bars to illustrate what he meant. 'No, I don't think we shall have to worry too much about Tommy spies during our trip through Lorraine,' Colonel Stuermer concluded. 'Now then, gentlemen, this is what we are going to do in Metz . . .'

But Colonel Stuermer was mistaken in his belief that the Resistance was not active in Lorraine. As the first of the disguised S-boats began to nose its slow way down the centre of the channel past Sierck-les-Bains, eyes were already following its progress with lively curiosity.

Henri Held, the youngest member of *'Réseau Boche'* – so-called because all the members of this most easterly of the great network of SOE* *réseaux* spoke German as their first language – had been watching the shipping that came up and down the Moselle for ten months now, ever since the 'chain-dogs' had dragged his father away for service in the *Wehrmacht*. In the months that had passed since that terrible morning when the German military police had beaten his father into insensibility, the pale-faced 16-year old had been able to pass on a great deal of information to the Baron.

Now, with the door of the book-filled storage room firmly closed behind him, he stared with growing interest at the four little ships sailing steadily down the centre of the river, well away from the coal barges plodding slowly up-stream, laden to gunwhales with the product of the Lorraine mines.

At first sight, they appeared to be tugs, but it was ob-vious from their wakes that they had more powerful engines than would normally be required on the slow-moving Moselle. There was something strange about them. For a while, as the four craft began to disappear round the great curve that the Moselle makes beyond Sierck, he could not make out what it was.

Then he had it! Although their decks were unburdened by any unusual weight and their crews seemed to be

*Special Operations Executive, a wartime British intelligence unit.

limited to the usual number, each one of them was riding deep in the water, as if their holds were heavy with some hidden cargo. The pale-faced young schoolboy bit his bottom lip. What kind of cargo would a tug carry? And why hide it below decks?

But before Henri Held had further time to ponder the question, there came the sound of a rusty old window being forced open next door and the reedy voice of old Koenigs, the Latin master, was crying angrily: 'Why the devil are you pissing out there for so long, Held? . . .Come on now hurry it! You'll never pass your *bach* like this!'

Henri Held, who would not live long enough to tackle the all-important examination, fled.

TWO

'The Baron will see you now, boy,' the ancient servant in his black suit announced, indicating the open door with his skinny hand.

'Thank you, Maurice,' Henri Held said grandly. 'You may retire now. We will not require you any further this evening.'

'I'll clip your ear for you in half a minute,' the servant quavered, swiftly dropping his High German accent and reverting to the Lorraine German dialect of the area.

Henri grinned and passed through the door into the study where the Baron – if he really were a Baron – a little, bald old man sat crouched over a map in his bath-chair, his false teeth carefully placed on the table next to him.

'Ah the boy,' he said with difficulty through ancient lips, wrinkled like prunes and turned inwards on the toothless gums. 'Sit.'

The teenage spy sat. A long time seemed to pass. Finally the Baron looked up and said hoarsely, 'You've come to tell me about the boats, I presume?'

Henri Held looked startled and the Baron chuckled throatily and then lapsed into a fit of coughing which left him red-faced and spluttering. 'Forgive . . . forgive me,' he gasped. 'Old men like to surprise the young, if they can . . . It's all they have left to them.'

'But how did you know *Monsieur Baron*?'

'I have another man at Diede' – he caught himself in time and deliberately used the French name for the border town at Thionville*. 'You don't need to know his name. He, too, was suspicious.'

'Their displacement—'

'Exactly, why should those tugs displace so much water? What kind of cargo do they carry, eh?' He looked shrewdly at the pale-faced boy.

'That was what I thought, Baron,' Henri said a little sulkily, put out by the fact that he was not the only one to have spotted the tugs.

'Come here, boy,' the Baron ordered and crooked a dirty forefinger at him.

Obediently he rose and crossed over to the Baron. Henri peered over his frail hunched shoulder at the map. '*Réseau Boche*,' he quavered, stabbing the map in the Moselle area, 'up to Metz . . . *Réseau Juggler* up to Epinal.' He stabbed the map again, as if he were trying to bore a hole through it. '*Stockbroker*, the most aggressive of the *réseaux*, located between Epinal and Chalon-sur-Saône.' He looked up suddenly. 'Is that clear, boy?'

'Yes sir,' Henri said a little hesitantly, wondering why such a newly recruited member of *Réseau Boche* as he should be told such important information.

'Now then, boy, we all know what kind of weak sisters those people down around Nancy are. They won't do anything. But the Burgundians are a different proposition. By evening those tugs will have passed out of our territory, but according to my calculations they should begin moving into the Stockbroker area by tomorrow evening. Now I should like the Burgundians to give them a warm welcome.'

*The German name of Thionville is Diedenhofen.

'How?'

The Baron did not reply directly to Henri's question. Instead he asked one of his own. 'My boy, how would you like to miss school for the rest of this week? Don't worry about the *lycée*. Koenigs' – he chuckled, 'Yes he is one of us – he'll fix school for you. I'll take care of your mother . . . But not the way you might think,' he added hastily and, as far as Henri was concerned, mysteriously.

'But what do you want me to do?'

'I want you to go south and contact Stockbroker.' He rapped the map with a skinny finger. 'This farm here, four kilometres south-east of Dôle on the Doubs is where you will find them, Henri. You see before the Germans marched into Vichy France it was the last staging post before crossing the demarcation line. Our friends made considerable use of it.'

'And how will I get there, Baron?'

'You will break the curfew tonight in a *gazogene**, which I will provide to take you as far as Dijon. From there you will go the rest of the way by bus and on foot. The driver of the *gazogene* needs only to know so much. You understand?'

'I understand,' Henri replied a little breathless and confused at the speed at which things were moving, but not afraid; he was too excited to be afraid. 'But what am I supposed to do when I reach Stockbroker, Baron?'

'You will give them an exact description of those four boats and you will help to identify them in due course. In other words, Henri, you have now become operational.' The grey sunken eyes of the old man became mesmeric in their intensity. In his cracked voice, he said : 'Soon boy, you will experience your baptism of fire. It will be a frightening, but glorious moment. I experienced mine when I was not much older than you at St Privat in '70. Yes, boy, I am that old !† But I remember it as if it were yester-

*A wood-burning car.

†St Privat, a battle of the Franco-Prussian War 1870, just outside Metz.

51

day. A glorious, glorious moment.' With a hand that trembled violently he reached in the drawer of the table on which the map lay and brought out a little pistol. 'My silver lady,' he announced, raising it to the lamp so that its barrel gleamed in the yellow light. He fondled it as if it were some living thing. 'She is my last remaining mistress,' he crooned, 'and like most mistresses she is highly dangerous when loaded!'

With difficulty he removed the magazine from the butt and took out one of the bullets. 'Look,' he said, 'dum-dum ammunition.' Henri, his brain racing now, craned his head forward. The soft nose of the 9mm slug had had a cross carved into it. 'Why the cross, sir?' he asked.

The Baron beamed at him. 'So, my gallant boy, the bullet will disintegrate the moment it strikes anyone. That mite of a thing will stop a giant at twenty metres. It should. It can cause a hole as big as my fist and, boy, it is yours from now onwards. From this moment, my silver lady is yours. I hope you will honour and treasure her. Here.'

'Thank you, sir,' Henri said, hesitantly pocketing the pistol and wondering if he dared ask how one fired such a thing.

'Don't mention it, my boy,' the Baron said, bringing his face close to Henri's so that the latter could smell his fetid breath and decaying body. 'Go now . . . go now, Henri. And remember,' his cracked voice rose shrilly, *'it is for France!'*

THREE

'Ay-ouch-nem! Ay-ouch-nem! Let us pull together, boys, pull once more . . . *Ay-ouch-nem!'* Ox-Jo sang the 'Volga Boat Song' in atrocious Russian as he and a handful of Stormtroop Edelweiss men under his command strained at the lock windlass.

All day they had been sailing through the flat French countryside between lines of still poplars, past golden, freshly cropped wheatfields. By evening the character of the countryside had begun to change. It had become hillier, with patches of fir forest on the heights and the parched brown fields were more often than not filled with short, stubby vines.

The river-canal system was becoming more complicated too as they edged closer to the Rhône. Now as they passed Chalon-sur-Saône and began to approach the Gigny *barrage*, which they must pass before entering the Rhône, they started to run into a series of locks which reduced their speed to walking pace.

Now, just as the light had begun to fade, they had been stopped by another lock. Ox-Jo had been forced to go into action again. Thus, he and his men manned the hand gears and strained at the mechanism which would set the gates in motion and allow them to pass through into the eight chambers of the lock.

The S-boats floated quickly on the mirror-like surface of the river. Apart from Ox-Jo's song, the heavy evening silence was broken only by the croak of the frogs and the whir of the invisible insects, skidding across the still expanse of water. The little fleet was becalmed, and suddenly very vulnerable.

From far away came the sad night sound of a train whistle. Henri Held, dressed now in a pair of workingman's overalls, rubber-soled shoes and with his face blackened, started.

The Englishman, or 'the Yid', as his French followers called him behind his back on account of his obviously Jewish features, pressed Henri's arm reassuringly. 'It's all right, kid,' he said 'everybody gets the wind-up the first time.'

Henri squirmed round and stared at his companion's sly face among the thick ferns lining the bank and said in the bravest voice he could muster, 'Don't worry about me, Englishman.' He flourished the 'silver lady'. 'I'll be all right.'

The Englishman ducked his head to one side swiftly as if

he half-expected Henri to pull the trigger of the fancy woman's pistol, and said, 'Of course, you will, kid. Of course!' Then he turned his attention to the four boats down below.

He had been dropped the previous August, prior to the Allied landing in Sicily, to disrupt water traffic through France just when the Germans would have most need of it. As the Allies had moved from Sicily to the mainland, and the Germans started to rush their E- and S-boats, miniature submarines and supply transport of all kinds southwards, he and *Réseau Stockbroker* had gone into action.

First it had been the Briare Canal locks, then the Mauvages locks on the Marne-Rhine Canal west of Toul. Soon it would be the Gigny and Port Bernalin *barrages* on the Seine-Rhône Canal and that would mean a total, if temporary, blockage of the whole French waterway system. As he lay in the damp ferns, the ambitious ex-salesman told himself that if he succeeded it would mean the Military Cross and *Croix de Guèrre* for him and possibly promotion to major. That should be sufficient to ensure his elevation to a managerial position in his firm's Leeds factory after the war!

The lock-keeper was out of the way, forced to return home by a sudden attack of diarrhoea, brought on by the sight of a sten-gun pointed straight at his guts. One of the *réseau* who was an electrician had cut off both the electric power to the lock-keeper's post and the quay-side telephone, used by bargees in trouble at night. The platoon of hated *Milice** guarding Gigny *barrage* itself would arrive on the scene too late to help the Boche down below once the attack went in. As for the elderly German soldiers of the transport unit stationed at nearby Thorey, they were already snoring drunkenly in their beds, or otherwise occupied in the town's one brothel – the *réseau* had seen to that.

The Englishman glanced at the men crouching around

*The Vichy-raised para-military police force which helped the Germans.

54

him in the undergrowth and whispered, 'Once they're in the lock,' he slapped the big 25 litre oil drum at his side, 'then we let them have it.' He grinned at the scared youngster who had brought the message from *réseau Boche*. 'Don't look so glum, lad,' he said encouragingly. 'We're going to have a party tonight, complete with bonfire. You're going to love it!'

'Switch on running lights, *Obermaat*,' *Korvettenkapitan* Doerr ordered.

The petty officer flicked a switch. Lights went on to port and starboard and at the stern and glowed in the grey mist.

Doerr sniffed. A pale moon was beginning to ascend above the poplars, but its light was still shadowy and un-certain. It would be tricky edging the twenty-five metre S-boats through the lock without the skilled assistance of the lock-keeper. Still it had to be done if they were to reach the sea in time. 'All right,' he commanded, 'both ahead. Dead slow!'

'Both ahead. Dead slow it is, sir,' the helmsman answered and eased the twin throttles forward gently.

Slowly the boats began to edge their way into the lock, while Ox-Jo and his men waited to close the gate behind them.

The minutes passed leadenly, while Doerr ran from side to side of the makeshift bridge checking the clearance, and the helmsman sweated at the controls. Behind them the other three boats, their engines chugging throatily, began to nose in behind.

Stuermer and Greul had decided that it was dark enough for them to go on deck and, standing well clear of the sweating sailors, they watched the tricky operation with interest and impatience.

'What do you think, Colonel?' Greul broke the silence.

Stuermer shrugged in irritation. 'God knows! I'm a lay-man in these matters. All I'm concerned with is that we get through this damned waterway system without being spotted.' He sighed angrily. 'I had never realized before just how many Frenchmen there were in the midst of a total war who had enough time off to go fishing! Any one of them could have been a spy for the Maquis!'

'A game they play here in France to justify their own cowardice, weakness and defeatism,' Greul sneered. 'Imagine what their big-mouthed politicians would make of it after the war if the Fatherland were ever defeated!'

'Of course,' Stuermer echoed woodenly, his mind already on the dangers inherent in their present position. Four boats immobilized in the narrow lock, far away from any German military establishment in this remote, God-forsaken corner of France, with the mist thickening. For all he knew, the banks on both sides might be full of armed partisans. It was an ideal spot for an ambush. 'Greul,' he snapped suddenly above the abrupt roar of the water rushing into the lock, 'I want you to do something . . .'

Using the traditional French infantry hand signals, the Englishman directed his men to their positions. Like trained killers, instead of the peasant irregulars that they were, they glided to left and right noiselessly through the wet mist. The Englishman turned to the boy who knelt at his side bewildered and now for the first time really scared. The Boche were only twenty-odd metres away!

'Listen, lad,' he whispered urgently, 'keep beside me and I'll see you come to no harm.' Henri opened his mouth to protest; then thought better of it.

'When I give the signal, grab hold of that drum.' He indicated the 25 litre drum standing behind the nearest tree, 'and give it one hell of a push down the slope.'

'But why?'

'Why? So we can give the Boche a nice warm welcome. The drum is watertight and full of an oil mix – a kind of oversize Molotov cocktail. With a bit of luck it should bump right against that leading boat. Then all hell will break loose.'

'But how are you going to detonate it?' Henri asked.

'Let that be my worry. Concentrate on your own job.'
Holding his sten gun firmly in his right hand, the Englishman pulled a small grenade from his pocket and glanced
at his men. Satisfied, he turned to Henri again, 'Get ready,'
he snapped.

'Ready!'

NOW!

Henri heaved. The heavy drum crunched through the
bushes and rolled down the slope, gathering speed at every
moment.

'FIRE, YOU BLOODY IDIOTS!' the Englishman
roared.

The riverbank erupted in a ragged volley of small arms
fire. Lead thwacked into the wooden sides of the German
boats. Spurts of water shot up everywhere around them,
and then the oil drum struck the surface and drifted towards the leading boat.

The Englishman ripped out the pin of the grenade and
pitched it towards the drum. Metal struck metal. *Crump!*
The grenade exploded in a shower of burning white phos-
phorus and with a great whoosh, the canister caught fire,
burning away the mist in a flash. Flaming scarlet, it struck
against the side of the leading S-boat and splashed burning
oil all over its bows.

'Got the bugger!' the Englishman cried exuberantly, as
the S-boat began to burn and frenzied dark figures came
into the range of the small arms fire of the waiting Resistance men. 'Got him!' – The words died on his lips. The
decks of the other boats were flooded with men. Wild pistol
and rifle shots began to stab the air and he could hear the
high-pitched hiss of a Schmeisser machine-pistol coming
from further up the basin.

'They're not sailors!' he cried. 'Come on, lads, let's get
the hell out of here! Come on!'

His men broke from their positions. Zigzagging crazily,
they dodged the concentrated fire which was pouring in
from below. At his side, Henri Held, his face ashen, his
legs trembling with fear, could hear the enemy bullets his-

57

sing through the trees all around him, as the vicious snap-and-crackle of the small arms fire rose to a peak.

Suddenly the Englishman seemed to notice him. 'What the devil are you still standing there for?' he shouted, swinging his sten gun from side to side, hosing his front with fire. 'Take off you silly young bugger!'

Henri was rooted to the spot with fear. There was nothing glorious about this moment, as the Baron had promised there would be; he experienced nothing save absolute, overwhelming terror.

'Move it!'

'I can't,' he quavered.

'You silly bastard,' the Englishman cried. He freed a hand and slopped Henri hard across the face. 'Now bugger off before—' His words ended in a shocked gasp of pain as the first slug hit him in the face. He slumped to his knees, sten still clasped in hands, his face abruptly transformed into a mess of broken bone and blood.

'Go . . . For Chrissake!' Automatically he squeezed the trigger of his sten. The slugs dug a sudden furrow, only metres in front of him. He had been blinded!

Henri Held screamed and leaving the Englishman firing wildly at an enemy he could not see, he ran through the trees, blundering wildly from side to side as bullets followed him like red-hot, angry fireflies.

'*Achtung!*' Ox-Jo snapped from the position behind the railway embankment to which Colonel Stuermer had ordered them fifteen minutes before. 'Here come the treacherous Frog bastards!'

The six troopers of the shore party raised their automatics. 'Fifty metres,' Ox-Jo ordered, as cool as if he were back on the range at Kufstein. 'Hold it . . . hold it now,' he added warningly.

'Shouldn't we fix bayonetes?' Jap whispered. 'In a minute we'll be able to bayonet 'em.'

'I'll bayonet your asshole, if you don't shut up,' Ox-Jo hissed. 'Thirty metres.'

Now they could see the twenty-odd civilians quite clearly. Most of them had thrown away their weapons, but still they outnumbered the Stormtroop Edelweiss men, three to one.

'NOW!' Ox-Jo roared and his men fired their first volley. The fleeing Frenchmen were stopped dead as if they had run into an invisible wall. Most went down in the first volley, lying where they fell in the suddenly bloody grass. A few of the survivors tried frantically to break away and run for cover.

The Edelweiss men did not give them a chance. 'Individual targets;' Ox-Jo commanded and, without appearing to aim, he shot a Frenchman in the back. He slammed into the nearest tree as if kicked by a mule and slithered the length of its trunk, dragging a bloody trail along the bark. Eagerly the mountaineers sprang to their feet from behind their cover and started picking off what was left of *Réseau Stockbroker*.

Henri Held, running desperately for cover, blood streaming down the side of his face from a bullet wound, paused and attempted to fire. A Boche slug struck the silver lady, just as he was about to press the pistol's trigger, and hauled it to the ground.

But it was too late. What was left of the Resistance group were halting where they stood and raising their hands above their bowed heads in token of surrender. *'Kamerad!'* they were beginning to cry in hoarse fear. *'Kamerad -nix schiessen!'*

Slowly the 16-year old youth began to raise his hands too, realizing numbly that he had just been condemned to death.

FOUR

'Well?' Colonel Stuermer demanded urgently, as the sweating sailors and soldiers beat out the last of the flames caused by the burning oil.

Korvettenkapitan Doerr, who had plunged fully clothed into the water to assess the damage to his ship, looked up at him and said, 'Toss me down a rope, Colonel, and I'll tell you the good news. That shitting bomb or whatever it was didn't hole her. We can sail on !'

'Thank God for that !' Stuermer breathed. 'But will she stand up to the sea once we're in the Med ?'

'I should imagine so. If not, your mountain men better start learning to swim quickly.' He grinned, but in the light of the dying flames Stuermer could see that his eyes remained worried. 'What's the problem?' he asked swiftly.

'The bomb burned the wooden cover off the torpedo tubes and the teak flanges have gone. Thank God, the fish weren't armed ! The whole boat would have gone up in the air. But now the dumbest of Frog agents could spot us for what we are – a German S-boat. Our silhouette is unmistakable.' He ran his forearm across his brow to wipe away the water dripping from his hairline.

Stuermer nodded his agreement dourly. The S-boats had a distinctive low and lean shape, which contributed greatly to their seaworthiness and speed. With the bow camouflage burned away, any enemy agent who had familiarized himself with the recognition tables of the German *Kriegsmarine,* would be able to recognize the boat at a glance. 'Do you think we'll have problems on the Rhône because of it?'

'Not on the Rhône, Colonel. In the Med ! If one of their agents reports to London that he has spotted four German S-boats heading for the Med, you can imagine what will be waiting for us when we emerge into the sea at the *Bouches de Rhône* . . . A bloody big British destroyer !'

'Let's hope you're being unduly pessimistic, Captain. All right, get ready to move off as soon as we're out of the lock. And there's no need to keep at reduced speed now, if anyone can spot us for what we really are. Get her up to the highest speed you can safely manage in the dark.'

'Right Colonel. We'll be under way as soon as your people open the other lock gate.'

'I'll see to it personally. Major Greul is up there with

the shore party.' Colonel Stuermer tapped his holster as if to reassure himself that it still contained his pistol and sprang the three metres from the bow of the S-boat to the concrete jetty.

He walked swiftly along the jetty in the direction from which moaning was coming. Suddenly a cry of fear and the dry crack of a pistol rang out. He hurried forward. Major Greul was standing in a circle of blue light thrown by Sergeant-Major Meier's torch, pistol in hand, a look of contempt on his face, staring down at the body of the man he had just shot.

'Greul, did you shoot that man?' Stuermer cried in a shocked voice. The Major looked at him calmly. 'I did Colonel,' he answered, his voice its usual dispassionate tone.

'But he was a prisoner, man!'

'I know, Colonel. But what are we to do with them? We can't take them with us. And God knows where the nearest German troops are in this area?'

'The French authorities,' Stuermer said, desperately searching for some solution to the prisoner problem and knowing there was only one – Greul's. 'There'll be a garrison of Darlan's *Milice* in the nearest town. Perhaps at Lyons.'

Greul made no attempt to conceal the sneer in his voice. 'Hand them to the French, Colonel? Why that's tantamount to setting them free. There are traitors to the German cause everywhere – even among the *Milice*. No – there is only one way with them. This!' he slapped his pistol with his free hand. Stuermer swung round. One of the prisoners – a boy with a wound in his head – had begun to sob. Perhaps he had understood the German. 'Stop that!' he commanded.

Henri Held continued to sob and he was still crying when Major Greul placed the cold muzzle of his pistol behind the boy's right ear and blew him into extinction.

The final pistol shot seemed to echo on and on for ever, while the little group of troopers stared numbly at the heap of broken bodies. Then Greul snapped, 'Well, Colonel, what are we to do with them? Leave them here as a warning to the rest of that decadent French pack?'

Stuermer pulled himself together, repressing the sense of self-loathing that he felt. 'No,' he said throatily. 'No, we cannot do that. I'm sure there are others still alive who know of this group. Sooner or later they'll come looking for them, and we don't want them finding the bodies until the S-boats are out to sea.' He raised his voice. 'Meier.'

'Sir?'

'Get your party to attach a weight to each body. I'll get another party ashore to deal with the lock.'

'Yes sir. And then sir?'

'Dump them in the water,' Stuermer snapped, deliberately making his voice cold and unfeeling. 'Now come on Greul, we've got a lot to do.'

They sailed steadily southwards all night, passing through Lyons without difficulty. The curfew held the city in its sway. Blacked out and silent, the only traffic moving on the Rhône was that sanctioned by the German authorities. Valence went by. The river became broader, and occasionally through the low-lying mist the men on deck could catch vague glimpses of a strange, primitive world of rocky shores and sandy islands, shrouded in thick rushes. By turns the water was deceptively placid and savagely violent whenever the Rhône narrowed to pass through some narrower rocky gorge. But *Korvettenkapitan* Doerr, the only one of the little flotilla's officers to have navigated the Rhône before, kept his ship and the others following from running aground. But he could only do so at the cost of reducing speed.

Thus it was, as light gusts of wind began to blow the mist away to reveal the first dim glow of dawn, that they found themselves still some eighty kilometres from the estuary of the Rhône.

Standing next to Doerr, tired and unshaven at the helm, Colonel Stuermer frowned. But he said nothing to the sailor. They would let events take their course and chance what might well be waiting for them once they emerged into the open sea.

The hours passed. Now it was rapidly becoming light with that suddenness typical of the Mediterranean. The wind began to freshen. *'Mistral,'* Doerr commented, not taking his eyes off the flat sheen of glistening water on the horizon. 'It won't be long now before we're out of the river.'

'Excellent,' Stuermer said.

'Let's wait a while before we say that,' Doerr said dourly. 'We don't know yet who or what might be waiting for us out there, do we?'

Another half-hour went by. They were nearly clear of the river now. To both sides of the ever widening estuary were long stretches of dark yellow sands. The S-boat in the lead began to buck a little more wildly. Down below Ox-Jo started to change colour. Suddenly he bolted for the heads, crying at the laughing troopers, 'Make way . . . make way, I'm going to spill my cookies!'

Doerr handed over the boat to a petty officer and stood, legs braced against the sudden swell, searching the broad expanse of water to his front with his binoculars, while Stuermer and Greul waited tensely at his side for his decision.

He covered every metre of the horizon with infinite patience before finally lowering his glasses and announced, 'Not a Tommy in sight. We've made it!'

Stuermer beamed. 'And what now?'

'Well, in the old days we would have kept close to shore, before making a break for Sardinia. But God knows what the situation is since the Macaronis have thrown in their lot with the Tommies. I don't think we'd better head straight for Rhodes in the hope that the Tommy MTB squadron at Sicily is looking the other way when we come sailing by.' He raised his voice and shouted to the helmsman, *'Obermaat, voller Fahrt voraus!'*

'Jawohl, Herr Korvettenkapitan, voller Fahrt voraus!' the Petty Officer yelled back.

The banshee shriek of the three 6,150 hp diesel engines filled the morning world. The S-boat leapt forward. Stuermer felt the deck tremble madly beneath his feet and frantically grabbed for a support as the boat came up on its toes like a ballet dancer. Suddenly the water was flying by in a dizzy shoulder-high white blur. Doerr grinned at the two officers and cupping his hands around his mouth, he cried above the controlled duet of roaring engine and screaming water, 'Gentlemen, it's all yours. Wake me when we reach Rhodes.'

Grinning hugely, he staggered off down below where the green-faced mountain troopers were lining up to be sick. Rapidly the four little craft headed out to sea in a white V, as the coastline dwindled behind them and then disappeared over the horizon.

Lieutenant John 'Kiss-Me' Hardy waited until they were definitely out of asdic range before he ordered the midget-sub's periscope up once more. The circle of calibrated glass was empty. They had gone. 'Down periscope!' he commanded, suddenly very pleased with himself. After all, this was the first nibble he had had ever since he had sailed from Gib forty-eight hours earlier and taken up this position near the mouth of the Rhône. Whatever the four Hun boats were, they were definitely not the tugs they pretended to be. 'All right, Sparks,' he called across to the radio operator crouched behind him in the tight confines of the little submarine, 'I want you to raise Flag Officer, Sicily and transmit the following signal, "At exactly zero eight hours . . ."'

FIVE

The storm rose when they were still west of Sicily. It started slowly, building up to its full impact gradually. First the horizon darkened, black clouds tinged with the grey-white of the rain, rolling ever closer to the flotilla of little ships. Then the green sea became a sullen black, abruptly crested with snow-white angry mops. The rain followed. A miserable drizzle, which gradually transformed itself into a thundering downpour.

Now the storm mounted rapidly. The angry white crests thundered and battered at the S-boats. Waves swilled over the low deck, drenching the grim-faced sailors hanging on to any support for dear life. Below the boats echoed eerily to the repeating crashes of the huge waves, and to the green-faced soldiers it seemed that every blow was the last the boats could take.

But *Korvettenkapitan* Doerr had no intention of letting his or any of his S-boats sink. That long afternoon he brooked no defeatism on the part of his crew, as their spirits began to flag. He was everywhere, encouraging the weary men at the pumps or the frozen sailors on deck watch, bullying them too when necessary forcing them by sheer willpower to keep the boat afloat.

The storm worsened. The rain gave way to gusty squalls, which battered the little ships and made them appear to stagger and almost stop, with their screws churning purposely above the wildly heaving water. Time and time again the little ships seemed suspended in mid-air, before dropping deep into the trough of the bellying waves.

In the lead S-boat, Doerr took over the helm himself, fighting the wheel furiously, the veins standing out at his temples, as he battled to prevent the ship from being forced round to broadside, where she might well be swamped by the terrible weight of water.

He ordered the deck cleared of any unnecessary weight to reduce rolling. The drenched crew, wielding their axes in the squall's flurries as if they were trying to battle the rain itself, cut away a smoke float, a dinghy and other odd gear on deck. Still the S-boat was not answering as she should. 'Get rid of this damned camouflage!' Doerr bellowed, the howling wind snatching the words from his mouth. 'Come on, move you idle dogs!'

The fake bridge was chopped away. The long funnel followed and then the stern. The deckhands clutched the life lines with one hand and hacked at the wood with the other, wave after wave submerging their contorted bodies in green, churning fury.

Doerr achieved the desired results. The rolling began to diminish but still the storm raged in its full fury. His cap snatched off his head by the wind, Doerr fought the bucking wheel of his own ship, as the S-boat struck each new wave as if it were running into a brick wall. Slowly he began to lose hope. The S-boats were not designed for this kind of weather. The three skins of teak on a light metal frame would not be able to stand up to much more battering of this kind. Doerr began to pray for the first time since he had left his *Gymnasium*.

But then as rapidly as it had risen, the storm subsided. The howling wind diminished. Almost imperceptibly the horizon began to change from a frightening inky black to a leaden grey; and just when *Korvettenkapitan* Doerr had come to the decision that he must sacrifice his torpedoes to save his ship, it ceased altogether.

Soaked, dazed and exhausted, the young sailors staggered across the boats' decks to ascertain damage, while the miserable troopers below attempted to get to their feet on the swaying deck to clear up the vomit.

Doerr groaned with relief and handed the wheel over to a petty officer. He flexed his aching shoulders and wriggled his fingers, stiff and frozen from hanging on to the wheel so long.

'Do you Lords* subject poor stubble-hoppers like us to that kind of thing often?' Colonel Stuermer's voice queried from behind him.

Doerr spun round and grinned. The big mountaineer was definitely pale about the gills, although he was trying to put a brave face on it. 'You should see what we've got laid on for you later, Colonel,' he said.

Stuermer waved his hand urgently. 'No thank you! I'll

*Slang for Navymen.

66

forego any more little treats of that kind. Just get me and my chaps to Rhodes as soon as possible. Next time I'll fly.'

Before Doerr could respond, a frightened voice called from the littered deck below. 'Sir . . . sir! *Boat dead ahead, sir!*'

As one Doerr and Stuermer raised their binoculars. A dark shape smudged the horizon. And another! Colonel Stuermer tensed his back against the bulkhead and tried to steady himself, angrily wiping the salt water off the lenses of his glasses only to find them damp again a moment later.

Doerr was an old hand at this sort of thing. While Stuermer cursed and focused, fighting the movement of the little ship and the flying spume, the *Korvettenkapitan* slowly moved his more powerful glasses over the tumbling waves until finally the first ship slid into his view.

Visibility was lousy. For several minutes he could not make her out. Then suddenly the stranger's knife-like fo'c'sle rose clear of the water. For a moment the twin gun mounted just below the bridge was clearly visible. An instant later the boat plunged deep into the waves once again. But that moment sufficed. Doerr lowered his glasses, as if suddenly stung.

'*A Tommy! A Tommy motor gunboat!*' he cursed.

As more and more dark shapes appeared on the horizon, *Korvettenkapitan* Doerr hit the panic button. The klaxons screamed their shrill warning. Lieutenant Hardy's long vigil had paid off and the outnumbered S-boat flotilla had a fight on its hands . . .

SIX

'So this is the further surprise you promised us, Doerr,' Stuermer said. 'What now?'

'What now, Colonel? I'll tell you. Those craft out there,' he pointed to the four dark shapes forming up into an attack V, while the two others fell back to cover their rear, 'are Tommy motor gunboats, the largest of the English small boats. Not only have they got torpedoes as we have, they're each armed with a twin two-pounder gun.'

'I see,' Stuermer said 'and we've got nothing but your torpedoes?'

'Exactly.'

'And their speed?'

'Only five knots less than our own top – and I doubt if we'll be able to reach that, with your bunch of muscle-bound mountaineers weighing us down.'

'So what do you do?'

'Try to make a run for it. Once they get within torpedo range—' Doerr did not complete the sentence. Instead he thrust home the twin throttles. With a howl, its bow raising itself almost immediately out of the racing water, the leading S-boat shot forward.

Smacking wave after wave, she raced directly towards the advancing English. At 10,000 revs a minute, her impeller blades sucking in eighty tons of air every 60 seconds, she hurtled across the surface, trailing a great stream of water behind her.

Stuermer felt icy fingers of fear clutch at his guts, as the English craft grew ever larger. Suddenly he could see the Tommies quite clearly. Tiny figures running wildly for their posts. In the same instant a shell exploded in a burst of white water directly in front of the S-boat.

'*MGB, Green-one-one-zero!*' a bearded petty officer sang out below on the heaving deck.

While the torpedo-men crouched over their weapons, a rating at the S-boat's twin Spandaus pressed the trigger. Red and white tracer zipped across the surface of the water in a stream of deadly morse.

The leading Tommy fired again. Metal struck metal with a hollow boom. The S-boat staggered, as if it had run into something solid. Stuermer staggered back, blinded by a searing burst of flame. For one awful moment he thought they had been badly hit. But he was mistaken. Just as the torpedo-men fired their twin torpedoes, Doerr swung the wheel round.

With savage suddenness, the S-boat turned to port, her superstructure almost touching the sea. She catapulted forword in a long curving arc, the British shells peppering the water behind her harmlessly.

Stuermer swung round. The two torpedoes were rushing to their target, trailing frantic bubbles behind them. The British zigzagged madly, their formation opening up to allow the deadly fish to pass them.

At Stuermer's side, Doerr tensed, his lips moving soundlessly as he counted off the seconds. 'Now!' he cried eventually and slammed his fist down on the bulkhead. Nothing happened!

'Ach du Scheisse!' he cursed angrily, as the first torpedo missed. 'What are those damned torpedo-men doing with their fish—' The rest of his words were drowned by the crump of the second torpedo striking home. Suddenly the leading British craft ploughed to a stop. She began to burn immediately.

'Petrol engine!' Doerr cried exuberantly over the cheers of the crew. 'The Tommies don't have diesel like us.'

Stuermer watched transfixed, as the stricken craft spewed burning petrol into the water. She began to list to one side while survivors sprang screaming into the water, some of them already living torches themselves. With a great hiss, she slipped under the surface and was gone.

'Hurrah . . . hurrah!' the jubilant crew yelled, their faces gleaming with triumph.

'Knock it off,' Doerr cried urgently. 'Here they come again!'

A hollow, echoing boom . . . a tall column of water rose only twenty metres away. The S-boat rocked furiously while the gunners fired pitiful bursts with their machine-guns at the Tommies. 'Make smoke!' Doerr cried desperately.

A sailor ran to kick the tub-shaped smoke float overboard and behind them the other S-boats were doing the same.

Thick black smoke poured from the floats immediately, but at that speed and with the wind they engendered, the smoke screen was a useless form of cover. The enemy was still able to range in on them. Stuermer realized that if Doerr did not pull some sort of trick out of the hat soon, they were finished.

Doerr, however, was at the end of his tether too. In spite of the fact that his little flotilla was going flat out, the Tommies were keeping up with them. It could only be a matter of minutes now before the kill.

'Now what?' Stuermer asked, cupping his hands about his mouth against the whine and crump of the shells exploding all around them.

'Now we die!' Doerr cried back.

But that was not to be . . .

Suddenly the third S-boat broke formation. In a great white arc of water, it spun round and headed straight towards the British boats. Stuermer could see the twin torpedoes leap from its sides and flip into the water. But instead of breaking to port or starboard, the unknown skipper of the S-boat continued his run in, following his torpedoes home.

'You stupid, young bastard, Krause,' Doerr cried in both admiration and anger, 'break now – break now!'

But Krause did not break. He continued his suicidal lone attack on the Tommies.

Hurriedly the British boats swerved to one side to let the two ton torpedoes hurtle through their formation harmlessly, all their fire concentrated on this single attacker now. Krause's boat was hit in the bows. She began to take water, plunging heavily through every trough, sheets of spray flying high above her. Still her engineer kept up the revs, and she plunged on, her machine-guns blazing.

'Oh, my God, Krause,' Doerr groaned in despair. 'break now, will you! Before it's too late!'

But it was already too late for the young *Leutnant*. A burst of 2-inch shells struck the lone S-boat at point-blank range. The craft staggered and for one long moment was still. Then her whole bow flew high in the air. Dazed and incredulous, Stuermer watched as the first greedy flames began to claw upwards at the S-boat's superstructure, now a raging furnace.

Doerr, his flotilla drawing ever further away from the British watched through smarting eyes as the flames consumed the stricken boat, leaping up to burn away that proud swastika flag.

Then it happened. A deafening roar. A blinding flash. The boat disappeared in a vast pillar of water which rose a hundred metres into the air before falling slowly to the debris-peppered sea like the curtain coming down on the final act of some great tragedy.

Stuermer turned away, as the surviving S-boats raced for the safety of the horizon, the British shells falling harmlessly in their wakes. 'My God,' he said weakly, not able to look any longer at the empty sea where *Leutnant* Krause's boat had been.

Thirty of his men had disappeared with her. Now Stormtroop Edelweiss was down to exactly seventy men and the operation had not even begun!

Twenty four hours later the little flotilla began its approach to Rhodes. To the north-west the island of Kos was held by the British, thus they ran in along the south-west, watching the ancient Acropolis grow ever larger in the blood-red light of the setting sun.

'Phew,' Ox-Jo breathed as he lounged at the rail next to a pensive Jap, 'am I glad that we're getting off this tub. I never even want to see a glass of water again! What's up with you?' he grunted. 'I made a joke.'

'I heard you,' Jap answered morosely, as the S-boat's speed slackened and they prepared to enter harbour. 'And I'm laughing – *inside*.'

'All right, you little runt of a half-breed,' Ox-Jo growled, 'let's have it! What's worrying you?'

'Nothing's worrying me,' Jap answered, as the S-boat

glided silently by the mole lined with bored soldiers in faded khaki drill.

'Something must, or you wouldn't have a face like that, as if you've crapped in your pants.'

Jap rounded on the big man suddenly. 'Get off my back, Ox,' he snarled, his hand dropping to the little pocket in which the Sergeant-Major knew he concealed his curved Hunza knife. 'You know as well as I do what's wrong. This little effort's got a fucking jinx on it. First the business in France. Then the Tommies.' He licked his salt-caked lips. 'Ox, if you ask me, Stormtroop Edelweiss has let itself in for a right old rollicking on this one.'

Part Three

ATTACK ON MOUNT CLIDI

ONE

The operations room of General Mueller's headquarters was uncomfortable and airless, its low roof baking in the afternoon sun. The men of Stormtroop Edelweiss shifted on the high-backed wooden chairs in a vain attempt to get comfortable. Through the slatted wooden shutters came melancholic music from a nearby waterfront *taverna*. It irritated Colonel Stuermer. One needed to have an untroubled, easy mind to appreciate that kind of thing and at this moment he had never felt less untroubled in all his Army career.

He addressed his men sharply, 'General Mueller, commander of the invasion force, obviously intends to give us every chance of pulling this operation off.

'The General has found two island caiques for us. They are not S-boats, but I think they'll get us to Leros more silently and safely than the S-boats would.' He tapped the big map at his side with the fly-swatter. 'We shall sail up to the island from the south, along the Turkish coast and within Turkish coastal waters.'

'But what if we are challenged by the Turks, sir?' Greul objected quickly.

Stuermer took a gleaming gold coin out of his trouser pocket. 'A British sovereign. They tell me that they call them "the horsemen of St George" locally. Well, the "horsemen" apparently have more influence on the Turks than the Tommies. They'll buy our way out of that particular problem, if it arises.

'Once we get close to the island, we go in the rest of the way by sail. The less noise we make, the better. Their Navy is very active at night according to Intelligence. We will land naturally at night, up here just above Ag Marina near Alinda Bay. There are apprently no natural beaches there – they are on the other side of the island. It won't be easy.' He looked at his men's hard brown faces. 'In fact, it'll be damn tough. The cliffs there are fifty metres high and pretty steep. No problem, of course, in daylight. But at night with the possibility that there might be Tommies about, well . . .' he shrugged and left the rest of it to their imagination.

'To land at night where there's no beach, climb a fifty metre cliff carrying forty kilos of equipment with the possibility that there'll be some hairy-assed Tommy standing on top taking potshots at us, sir. It's not exactly ideal climbing, sir,' Ox-Jo ended, summing up the situation for them all.

'There's nothing perfect in this world, Meier,' Stuermer said, trying to smile, and knowing that that was the usual sort of unthinking reply that senior officers always gave their men when they were sending them to their death. Stuermer knew that his superiors subscribed to a creed of ruthlessness in order to succeed. Human life meant little to them. But it did to him. He did not think, even after four years of bloody war, that the lives of his fellow-men were his to take. He loved Stormtroop Edelweiss above all things.

He was not going to sacrifice their lives, if he could help it.

'Now,' he continued firmly. 'As soon as we have landed and scaled the cliffs we shall make our way to this area here, about a kilometre away from the objective. According to Intelligence, it is a stretch of rough country, covered with trees, and uninhabited. It would be an ideal place for us to lie up till night. By dusk, however, we must be in position at the base of Mount Clidi, ready to begin the ascent. Any questions so far?'

'Yes sir.' It was Jap. 'Do you think the Macaronis will fight.'

'We don't know, Corporal. They are the unknown quantity in this business. But their government has thrown its lot with the Tommies, so we can assume they will.'

'And even if they do,' Greul sneered. 'We've had to suffer them as allies for three years, let the Tommies suffer now. They'll piss themselves when they see German steel.'

'Maybe,' Stuermer said though sounding unconvinced. 'They've got a tremendous position up there on top of Mount Clidi.'

'Yes sir,' Ox-Jo broke in, 'what's this Mount Clidi like?'

'Well, it's not very high. Perhaps a couple of hundred metres. The front slope looking south is relatively easy. There's a mule track up there for the Italians to bring up their supplies. But they've got it covered by machine-gun and gun emplacements, barbed wire too. Naturally it's not the approach we can make if we hope to surprise them. We shall take the rear slope, facing north and it won't be easy.'

'Why sir?' someone asked. 'Two hundred metres isn't that much of a problem.'

'No, not under normal circumstances,' Stuermer agreed. 'But it's almost a sheer face and we can't rope together at night under the conditions we are to be subjected to.' He flipped back the map of Leros to reveal a large, slightly blurred picture of a rock face. 'One of our reconnaissance planes took this yesterday.' He stepped back so that they could see it more clearly.

Their reaction was as he expected. A few whistled in surprise, but most of his men stared at the blow-up in shocked silence. 'Yes I know what you're thinking,' he said hastily. 'But it isn't as bad as you may imagine.' Quickily he stepped in front of the photograph and said, 'If you look closely, you will see that there is a crack – here. It's not much but it's a start. After about twenty metres, you can see that the crack begins to widen. It's big enough to get your knee in and take off some of the strain.

'About twenty or thirty metres from the summit – here – the crack becomes a chimney, big enough even for you to fit your big rump into, Meier. Now once we're in that chimney, it should be plain sailing. That is as long as we remember to turn our backs to the smooth, overhanging wall and our faces to the one with the most holds.'

'And how will we know that, sir?' Greul snapped impatiently. 'That photograph reveals nothing, and it will be dark when we begin our ascent.'

'Agreed, Greul. But I shall lead. Where I go, you go.'

'But a commanding officer shouldn't play guinea pig like that!' Greul protested.

'Let that be my worry, Major,' Stuermer said easily. 'I've faced worse. Now, you must remember above all on a climb like this conserve your strength at the first stage and do not panic in the chimney. Once inside it, the secret is to stay cool and search for the slightest hold for both your hands and feet.

'We sail tomorrow night,' he continued, his voice cold and unemotional, 'as soon as we have the cover of darkness.' Next door the music ended. Suddenly there was no sound in the big room save the heavy ticking of the old clock on the wall.

TWO

Stuermer breathed in deeply, savouring the salt tang of the sea and heavy scent of honeysuckle. From far off came the steady melodic tinkle of goat bells; the local peasants were bringing down their animals from tht hillsides for the night. Soon it would be time to sail.

He swung round and stared at the two shabby caiques, already warming up their ancient engines. They looked no different from the score or so he had seen since they had arrived at Rhodes. Weather-beaten, their paint peeling in long scabs, any casual observer would take them for a couple of local fishing craft or small traders about to leave on a night trip to another island or an offshore fishing ground.

But these two particular boats were crewed by a group of *Kriegsmarine* volunteers, dressed in a villainous assortment of civilian cast-offs. Below their crowded decks, their holds were packed with men and equipment, weapons,

78

stores and climbing gear. If they were stopped by a British naval patrol, there would be no hope of trying to bluff it out. They would have to fight; for as Mueller had told him only half an hour before, 'Stuermer, everything now depends on you and your troopers. You mustn't be taken before the main landing, or that will give the whole op away. In essence, Stuermer, you and your men must disappear now for the next fifty-odd hours. When you reappear, it must be at the top of Mount Clidi. If you can't make that objective, Stuermer, disappear – for good!' If they run into trouble, Mueller wanted him to fight to the death.

Unconsciously Stuermer shook his head and walked to the leading caique, where the captain, a petty officer from Hamburg's waterfront, was waiting for him. 'We're ready to go, sir, if you are.' With a wave of his hand he indicated the throaty, laboured noise of the engines below.

'Don't worry, sir,' he said reassuringly. 'They've been taking this old tub up and down the Aegean for the last fifty years. I imagine they'll last another twenty-four hours.'

'They'd better,' Stuermer said and went below.

For most of that night, the two caiques sailed steadily along the Turkish coast within Turkish waters. The sea was an incredible dark blue, the iridescent rippling of the gentle waves fanned by a scent-laden breeze. There was no sound save the steady beat of the engines, and the war seemed a thousand kilometres away.

The hours passed. At four, the petty-officer acting as captain asked Stuermer's permission to leave Turkish territorial waters and begin the approach to Leros. The Colonel gave it and had the men wakened. Now the dark rugged shape of the island they were to invade started to loom up on the horizon. They swung into a bay. The caique was beginning to rock a little with the surge of the sea against the land. 'Alinda Bay,' Major Greul said softly.

'Yes. That must be the little town over there,' Stuermer answered, indicating the silent white houses, half hidden by cypresses and pines which grew right down to the edge of the water.

'At least the Tommies there are fast asleep,' Greul said.

'Yes, so it seems. Let's hope it's that way all along the coast,' he added, feeling an eerie sense of foreboding as the wind whispered through the trees and above them the clouds scudded through a pale, ghost-like sky. He shivered suddenly.

'What is it, Colonel?' Greul asked.

'Nothing. Just a louse running across my liver.'

They sailed ever closer to that rocky forbidding shore. The caique was rocking wildly in the current now. 'It's going to be tricky, Colonel,' the petty officer cried, from where he wrestled with caique's wheel. 'As soon as I bring her alongside and broadside on, the tide's going to bang her hard. It'll be difficult to keep her steady for long.'

'Do the best you can, Petty Officer,' Stuermer cried above the slap of the waves against the base of the cliff. 'Remember my boys have forty kilos of equipment on their backs. They're going to get more than their feet wet if they go into the drink with that lot on their backs.'

The petty officer brought the first caique round parallel to the shore. The little boat started to yaw and plunge wildly, as she took the full impact of the waves broadside on. Sailors ran swiftly to the side nearest the cliff and tried to fend her off with their boathooks.

'That's about as good as I can do, sir,' the Petty Officer cried, as the first of the boathooks snapped like a shell exploding and the sailor holding it caught himself from falling into the tide.

'All right, Petty Officer, do your best!' Stuermer called, strapping on his rucksack laden down with explosives and personal effects, and slinging his carbine over his shoulder. He balanced himself on the swaying deck and tried to assess the situation. Above the white, phosphorescent line of foam he could just make out the first hold – a small ledge about three metres above the water. Under normal circumstances, he could have managed a thing like that with his eyes closed and one hand tied behind his back. But now he must attempt to fling himself onto it with forty kilos of equipment on his back as the caique rode the crest of the wave. The little ledge seemed as far away as the moon.

Stuermer drew a deep breath as the caique rose on the swell and he bent slightly, hands held taut to his sides. Then in one convulsive leap he launched himself forward into the darkness.

His knees crashed against wet rock. His hands shot out, fingers already extended. A nail ripped away as he clawed the sharp edge of the ledge. He screamed with pain. But fumbling frantically, he held on with a single hand. The heavy weight of his rucksack tore cruelly at his shoulders, trying to drag him down into the raging sea below. With what seemed infinite slowness he brought his left hand up and hooked his fingers over the lip of the ledge.

The rucksack seemed a ton weight, but he continued his painful progress upwards, red-hot pincers of agony nipping at his shoulders. Behind him the caique danced back and forth on the waves like a crazy cork. Stuermer got one booted foot on the ledge but he still had the whole of his weight and the sodden rucksack to drag upwards.

'Come on, Colonel,' Ox-Jo cried, digging his nails into his palm till it hurt, 'get the lead out of your arse! *Get up there!*'

And then Stuermer had done it and was lying pressed to the wet rock, heart beating like a trip-hammer, his breath coming in harsh shallow gasps.

He knew he had no time to rest. Ignoring the burning pain in his fingers, he fumbled with the flap of his rucksack. He took out his looped hammer and the alloy steel pegs. Swiftly he hammered in the pegs and attached the fine kernmantel rope. 'All right,' he yelled through cupped hands, 'I'm going to cast the rope! Major Greul, you first.' He glanced through the flying spray at the second caique, and breathed a silent prayer of thanks. His troopers had found a convenient rock near the wildly heaving little craft and were jumping for it and the shore, one by one, with comparative ease.

The white rope snaked through the air towards the crazily heaving caique which threatened to smash against the dripping rock wall at any moment. Greul caught it expertly. Stuermer took the strain. Greul launched himself forward high into the air. He landed nimbly on the ledge next to Stuermer who yelled above the wind, 'You're in charge now, Greul! I'm going on! Send them up behind me as they make the ledge.'

'But—'

Colonel Stuermer was no longer listening. He was already reaching forward into the dripping, inky gloom for the next hand-hold.

THREE

Stuermer paused, his chest heaving with effort, his lean body contorted in a vertical layback, left foot raised ready to move up and over the edge of the cliff. Below him he could hear the faint grunts of his men and the occasional noise made by metal striking stone, as they worked their way up the cliff face following in his tracks the best they could.

The climb had not been easy, but the suicidal risk he had been taking had been driven out of his mind by the knowledge that the sooner he had managed it, the sooner the agony would come to an end.

Now he was there and in spite of his exhaustion, not a little pleased with himself that he had managed it. But he knew there was no time to be wasted congratulating himself. With a grunt he raised himself over the edge of the cliff and sprawled full length in the damp, short-cropped grass.

Carefully and slowly, Colonel Stuermer searched his front – the spiked pines, the waving brushes, a cluster of what appeared to be boulders – while more and more of his men flung themselves over the edge of the cliff and lay there panting.

Suddenly he froze in heart-thudding immobility.

About fifty metres away a shadow had detached itself from the spiked pines. It moved slowly as if it were that of some bored, lonely soldier, performing a routine duty in the middle of the night and longing for a hot drink and his bunk. Whether the man out there was a Tommy, or some Greek curfew-breaker, he presented the utmost danger. He had to be eliminated. Swiftly Stuermer darted forward, trying not to lose the shadow.

He crawled closer. Now the shadow took on the recognizable shape of a British soldier. There was no mistaking that pudding-basin helmet and the rifle slung over his right shoulder. The Tommy was moving slowly forward about thirty metres away. He only needed to turn his head and surely he would see the dark shapes of the invaders crouched on the top of the windswept-cliff. Stuermer had to come in behind the Tommy and deal with him before he raised the alarm.

Stuermer broke right. His every movement was smooth, controlled and noiseless as he came up behind the unsuspecting man. He could make out the tails of the soldier's khaki greatcoat fluttering in the wind and the little pack hanging low on his shoulders making him look as if he had a hump-back.

Stuermer felt his stomach knot into a ball of writhing nerve ends. In spite of the cold wind, his body broke out into a sweat. He recognized the familiar symptoms : they were the ones which he always experienced before he had to kill.

He darted forward the last ten metres, taking no precautions now. The Tommy swung round. A torch flashed on illuminating a pale, frightened young face. What thoughts must be flashing through the boy's mind at this moment, surprised on the edge of a lonely cliff in the middle of the night by a man in German uniform ! The Tommy opened his mouth to shout. Stuermer gave him no chance. One hand shot up and knocked the torch to the ground. The other thrust back the Tommy's helmet. Like lightning Stuermer swung round the boy and grabbed his helmet. He pulled hard. The cry was stifled savagely in the boy's throat, as the webbing strap cut into his Adam's apple.

Stuermer thrust his knee into the small of the boy's back and increased his pull. Desperately writhing and wriggling, the Tommy tried to break that killing grip, his hands clawing at the strap cutting ever deeper into his throat.

Stuermer flung his own head back so that he could exert even more pressure. The boy was making awful little strangled noises now, his legs trampling the ground as he battled for air. Slowly, incredibly slowly it seemed to a wild-eyed, sweat-soaked Stuermer, the struggles became weaker and weaker until they ceased. Still Stuermer held his grip until he was quite sure that the Tommy would never breathe again. Then finally when the boy hung limply in his hands, he let go. The dead soldier slipped to the ground, leaving Stuermer standing there, trembling violently in every limb.

'You all right, sir?' It was Ox-Jo, moving forward remarkably silently for such a huge man. '*Sir,*' he said sharply, when Stuermer did not reply.

Stuermer took his eyes off the dead boy, trying to overcome his compassion for the silent figure, condemned to die on this god-forsaken cliff. 'Yes, thanks, I'm all right, Meier.'

'What shall we do with him, sir? I mean he's a dead give-away if his pals find—' Ox-Jo did not complete the sentence.

'Yes, I know,' Stuermer said, pulling himself together swiftly. 'We've got to make it look like an accident, just in case his comrades start looking for him. But how?'

'The cliff, sir.'

'What do you mean, Meier?'

'Well, sir on this kind of night with this wind, anyone could make a mistake and walk over the edge.'

'Right,' Stuermer said eagerly. 'That's it. Come on, Meier, give me a hand.'

The two of them bent and picked him up. Swiftly they moved to the edge of the cliff – the boy seemed to weigh virtually nothing – poised there, and then heaved together. The dead body hurtled into the night. They followed its progress for a fleeting second. Then the darkness had swallowed it up. Stuermer turned his head to the wind in order to catch the slightest sound. He thought he heard the splash of the boy hitting the water.

'Form up,' he ordered. 'At the double – come on now. We've no time to waste.'

The alpine troopers needed no urging. They knew the dangers; there might well be other Tommies out on patrol, in spite of what Intelligence in Rhodes had said to the contrary. At a rapid jog-trot they began to move inland, with Greul and young Lieutenant Sepplmayr bringing up the rear. Suddenly Sepplmayr stumbled and cursed out loud as he caught himself from falling just in time.

'*Schnauze, Sepplmayr!*' Greul hissed angrily. 'Do you want to wake the whole British Army!'

'Sorry, sir. I stumbled against something.'

'Oh, come on, you're damn clumsy, Sepplmayr.'

'Yes sir,' the red-faced Lieutenant answered unhappily and ran after the Major, leaving the sentry's torch undiscovered in the damp grass.

FOUR

The Dornier Do-217 K3s levelled off above Gurna Bay, breaking their formation slightly in order to launch their attack.

'They're armed with those bloody glider bombs again!' Colonel Tilney, the Fortress Commander, barked above the roar of flak coming up from the 3rd Light Anti-Aircraft Battery on Mount Meraviglia.

'Yes, I can just make them out beneath the wings of the

first Dornier,' Colonel French, the C.O. of the Royal Irish Fusiliers agreed, lowering his glasses. 'I think, Colonel, it would be wiser if we took our aged heads out of danger.'

'Agreed,' Tilney said, as the leading plane shuddered and seemed to stand still in mid-air. Next instant the Henschel glider bomb, carrying a ton of high explosive, shot from beneath its wing.

Hurriedly the two senior officers clattered down the stone steps into the command bunker, while the glider bomb began its flight towards the island in eerie silence. In a matter of seconds that silence would erupt into violent, ear-splitting destruction.

Tilney, a bronzed gunner, dropped on to a wooden chair and motioned the infantry colonel to do the same. 'A spot of whisky?' he asked above the racket of the anti-aircraft Bofors.

'Whisky! You are doing well up here, Tilney. We're down to that disgusting *ouzo* in the mess.'

'Rank hath its privileges,' Tilney said easily, pouring some of the precious ration whisky into a tin mug and passing it across to the other man. 'Cheers!' He raised his own chipped enamel mug.

'Cheers!'

A mile or so away the first glider bomb hit the island. The bunker shook violently in the explosion, but neither man seemed affected. They had both experienced enough bombing over these last months in the besieged island of Malta.

'Now,' Tilney said, as the Dorniers, having launched their glider bombs, came in for a strafing run before zooming away back to their bases at Rhodes. Everywhere on the Fortress heights, the brens and lewis guns opened up. 'What do you think, French. It's pretty obvious from that business outside that the Boche are softening us up for an attack.'

'Frankly I don't like it. I mean, I don't like your plan of defence. You are a gunner – and if you'll forgive me – you have the gunner's mentality.'

'And that is?' Tilney snapped.

'To dig in and go over to the defensive. The type of weapon you use dictates your attitude to battle. We in the infantry have a different concept.'

'Get on with it, French,' Tilney growled. 'What are you trying to say?'

'This. Our superiors have worked out a static defence plan for us, which I think impossible to carry out. We haven't the men and the coastline is too long and intricate to defend in its entirety.' He flung a challenging glance at the wooden-faced artillery colonel. 'What would happen if the Boche threw in an airborne attack in the centre of the island?'

'Impossible!' Tilney snorted. 'GHQ says that the hilly terrain makes it virtually impossible to land airborne troops on Leros. We would have done so ourselves if it had been possible. What we must expect is a seaborne landing. Once this softening-up show stops, they'll come in by sea.'

'You—'

French's words were drowned by the crump of a glider bomb crashing home somewhere on the island. Frantically he clutched his half-full mug of precious whisky as the underground room rocked with the force of the detonation. A wave of acrid cordite smoke swept through the bunker, setting the two of them coughing.

'Bloody Boche,' Tilney said, 'can't even let a chap drink his dinner in peace, what.'

'Exactly,' French replied and downed the whisky in gulp as if he were not going to take any more chances of losing it. 'Still, I don't agree with you about that seaborne landing.'

'What do you mean?'

Colonel French reached in the haversack buckled to his webbing belt and pulled out a torch, which he placed carefully on the rickety wooden table in front of the Fortress Commander, as if it had some very special significance.

Tilney looked at it. 'And what is that object supposed to signify, French?'

'One of my patrols found it this morning. It is all that is left of a certain Fusilier Kerrigan of my 'B' Company who was out with a roving patrol last night on the cliffs of Alinda Bay. We haven't discovered his body yet.'

'So? What happened – the poor chap walked over the edge of the cliff or something?'

'Could be. It was a very dark night and the top of the cliff up there is treacherous when it's wet, which it was last night.'

'Then why are you worrying me with the loss of one of your chaps and what the devil has it got to do with the overall defence of Leros?'

French leaned forward, fire in his dark eyes. 'Where we found the torch, we found the marks of many feet – boots, I should say.'

'What!'

'Yes. And I'll tell you something else, Tilney. One of my officers – a chap who was seconded to us from the Indian Army in the early days of the war and who was apparently a bit of a climber in the Himalayas before this show started – says they are the prints of a special sort of boot. He says that the tracks strike him as belonging to a "paidar" – a kind of simple leather boot worn in the Himalayas for climbing and fitted with a Swiss Luklein profile.

'The only people who could conceivably wear boots like that in Europe, apart from professional mountaineers, is the High Alpine Corps.'

'*Germans?*'

'Right in one,' French answered, his face grim.

Tilney looked at him aghast, realizing that the fact that there were possibly German troops already on the island proved just how wrong his all-round defensive plan really was. 'But what does it mean, French?'

'It means, Colonel that those mountain troops are here to prepare some sort of landing site for their paras – and it means too that we'd better find the buggers before it's too damned late . . .'

FIVE

'*Tommies, sir!*' the excited voice of the sentry whispered in Stuermer's ear.

He awoke at once, his body heavy and sticky with sweat in the late afternoon heat, his nose full of the heady odour of the pines among which they had hidden themselves. 'Where?'

'They're coming up the valley, sir,' the young trooper breathed softly, as if the English might well hear him.

Stuermer rubbed the sleep out of his red-rimmed eyes and parting the camouflage netting carefully peered down the valley.

It stretched before him in a perfect curve, closing in on both sides of the pine-covered slope on which the exhausted men of Stormtroop Edelweiss hid, apparently making their hiding place impregnable. But he – and German Intelligence – had been wrong. For as he wrinkled his eyes against the white glare of the burning sun, he could see the tiny black figures plodding purposefully down the length of the valley.

There were thirty or forty soldiers – perhaps a platoon – skirting the flank of Mount Clidi, searching behind each bounder, their bayoneted rifles held at the ready. The Tommies were looking for them!

'What now, Colonel?' It was Greul, all sleep vanished from his arrogant face, his usual super-efficient self. 'Do we fight? There are only a handful of them. Easy meat!'

'Entirely out of the question, Major! The mission comes first.' He looked up at the sun. It had fallen below its zenith, but it would be another three or four hours before it sank behind the mountain and darkness fell. He bit his lip and stared bitterly at the advancing British. Suddenly the inevitability of their approach was very frightening.

'Well?' Greul demanded. 'If we can't stand and fight, what do we do?'

Before Stuermer attempted to answer that unanswerable question, another voice broke in.

Stuermer spun round. It was young Lieutenant Sepplmayr. 'What is it, Lieutenant?' he asked impatiently. Sepplmayr was the last person he wanted to talk to at this particular moment.

'Sir, I've got an idea.'

'Save it,' Greul sneered. 'Treasure it for what it is – you don't have many of them, do you?'

Stuermer glared angrily as the young officer flushed hotly. 'What kind of an idea, Sepplmayr?' he asked a little more kindly.

'Well, sir, it looks as if they are searching for us. So why wait and accept the inevitable?'

'What do you mean?'

'Let them know we really are here.'

'Are you crazy?' Greul demanded angrily. 'You know our mission is not to be spotted till the attack starts.'

'I know, sir. I know. But let them see one man, let them chase him. Then they'll be satisfied. Perhaps they'll take him for some sort of saboteur landed to carry out a special mission. But they'll never know because they'll never catch him. And at all events, that lone man will draw attention away from the rest of the outfit.'

'And who is that particular hero going to be?' Greul asked. 'You, I suppose?'

'Yes sir,' Sepplmayr answered, his youthful face full of determination.

'And what do you propose to do exactly?' Stuermer asked, his mind beginning to race with new possibilities, new plans.

'Well, what would a saboteur do if he were spotted? He'd attempt to get back to where he had hidden the boat which had brought him to the island. So I would draw them back towards the sea, letting them see me naturally. Then when I was sure they were clear of this area, I'd head back up into the hills. I know I'm not the best of mountaineers, but I think I could easily disappear into those hills,' he indicated the ragged fringe of heights to their rear, their surface rippling bluely in the afternoon's heat haze, 'and work my way back to you.' He stopped abruptly and stared expectantly at his commanding officer.

Stuermer did not answer for a moment. Sepplmayr was neither a good mountaineer nor a particularly good soldier. A couple of times he had noted just how afraid the boy had been on a particularly dangerous stretch during their training climbs, just as he could see clearly that Sepplmayr was afraid now. But the young Lieutenant had stuck it out, although he was incredibly accident-prone, and that showed he had the guts of his peasant forefathers from the high mountains.

'All right, Sepplmayr. You can go. But I want you to take Meier and Corporal Madad with you. They are both highly experienced men.'

'Yes sir.' Stuermer could see the light of relief in the young officer's eyes; he wasn't going to have to do it alone after all.

'But know this, Sepplmayr. They might suspect you are German, but they don't know for certain and they *must not find out*!' He hesitated momentarily. 'If there is no other way out and you think you might be caught and made to talk, you—' he broke off abruptly.

'I understand, sir.' Sepplmayr touched his holster lightly, 'the officer's way out.'

'All right, Sepplmayr, so be it. Dump all equipment save your personal weapon.' Stuermer's voice softened and he clapped his hand on the young officer's thin shoulders, *'Hals und Beinbruch, Sepplmayr'**

'Thank you, sir.'

Five minutes later, the young Lieutenant and the two NCOs had broken cover and were running wildly across the rough ground heading for the coast.

It seemed to take the Tommies an age to spot their

*Roughly happy landings, literally 'break your neck and bones.'

flight. Then suddenly the long line of dark figures halted. There was a medley of orders and counter-orders. A rifle cracked. But the slug whistled harmlessly wide of the running men. Someone blew a whistle. Hurriedly the line shortened. And suddenly the Tommies, laden down with packs and steel helmets, were doubling through the pines to the left of the hidden men, in full chase.

Sepplmayr's opening move had paid off.

SIX

The British troops, more tightly bunched now, were straggling up the steep slope to the sea. Sepplmayr, crouched low in the gorse next to the two NCOs, could see that they were tiring rapidly. Their officer had to use his whistle repeatedly and every now and again his angry shouts were wafted across to them by the wind.

'Looks as if they're been doing more fucking than fighting, *Leutnant*,' Jap commented. 'The way they're floundering around down there.'

'Ay,' Ox-Jo growled, 'and you'd better thank your heathen gods they have, yer slant-eyed apeturd. Otherwise those Tommies would have had you for their five o'clock tea by now.'

'Shut up!' Sepplmayr snapped without rancour. He was beginning to enjoy the chase now, his fear overcome. 'All right,' he said finally. 'It'll be another couple of hours before it gets dark. So we're going to lead them a little dance around the coast for another thirty minutes before we disappear into the hills. By that time, it'll be near dusk and perhaps they'll think we've got away by sea.'

'Right, sir,' Ox-Jo agreed. 'What now then?'

'We show ourselves and then begin running again.'

As they broke cover, there was a shout of rage. The officer blew his whistle in a shrill peremptory blast. It echoed across the valley with imperative urgency and before it had died away, the British infantry had stumbled into a run and were in full chase once more.

Now the three running men were struggling along the edge of the cliff, the fierce sea-wind tearing at their clothes and making movement difficult. The Tommies were beginning to gain on them, but there was still a comfortable distance between the two groups. Behind them they heard the chatter of a sub-machine gun. Lead whined off the boulders to their right in a murderous ricochet. Sepplmayr ducked instinctively, fear shooting through his bowels. Then he forced a grin and told himself that he was in the company of two fine men. His courage returned and he staggered on. Now they were only a matter of metres away from the first of the scrub-covered hills, already veiled with the purple mantle of the approaching night. 'Up there,' he gasped. 'I think we can start losing them now!'

Ox-Jo and the Jap nodded their understanding. 'Watch it, sir,' Jap said. 'We'll have to slow down once we hit the slope.'

'I will, Corporal,' Sepplmayr answered. He understood immediately. For the first twenty odd metres of their climb, the advantage would be on the side of their pursuers. He glanced at the rock face to their front and worked out a route. 'To the left of that withered pine!' he gasped. 'It'll cover our backs – for a minute or two at least.'

A burst of sub-machine-gun fire ran in an urgent blue line along the rocks, as they began their climb. The sound of the Tommies grew closer. A rifle bullet hit the tree above Sepplmayr's head. He ducked. The severed branch missed him by centimetres. Fighting for breath, Sepplmayr looked over his shoulder. The Tommies were perhaps two hundred metres away now. Here and there soldiers had flung themselves to the ground and were taking more careful aim at the men on the hillside, while the rest hurried on.

Sepplmayr redoubled his efforts. Next to him, a sweating Ox-Jo was going up the rocks at tremendous speed for such a big man. Jap was equally swift and both men were taking

93

expert advantage of what cover there was. Sepplmayr realized he still had a lot to learn about mountain warfare.

Now the first of the Tommies had reached the foot of the hill and were beginning the climb. The fire of their comrades died away raggedly.

Slowly but surely the three mountaineers began to outdistance the unskilled English soldiers. They climbed higher and higher, followed by angry shots from the soldiers on the slope. Sepplmayr concentrated on climbing. To his left and far below, the sea stretched a perfect dark blue, its surface unmarred by a single sail. It looked beautiful, but the young Lieutenant had no time for its beauty. He concentrated on the purpose of their mission : to make the British believe they were heading for the sea. 'Bear left,' he called to the two NCOs who were now ahead of him 'Another ten minutes or so and it'll be dusk.'

'*Jawohl, Herr Leutnant,*' they called back in unison and began to tack across the hill-face in the required direction.

Sepplmayr followed, traversing the face without too much difficulty. Below them the sounds of their pursuers were becoming fainter. Sepplmayr stared up at the dark summit. Once they were over that they would be safe. Then it would be only a matter of sneaking back to the Stormtroop under the cover of darkness. There might even be a medal in this for him. Naturally it would not be as good as his father's Bavarian *Pour le Merite,* but it would be something to convince the old man that the youngest scion of the family was not all bad.

He reached up for the next handhold – a slab of what looked like slate. Then it happened. The rock broke off in his grasp. Instinctively his other hand clutched his waist-high handhold. To no avail. His fingers began to slip. He bit his lip to prevent himself from screaming out with fear. His hand came free. He slid down the hillside in an avalanche of rocks and stones, the rough surface ripping and clawing at his body cruelly, the noise the clattering stones made drowning the cries of pain emerging from his gasping lips. But their noise did not drown the scream of pure agony as he hit the ledge and his right leg broke with a crack like a dry branch underfoot in a hot summer!

'*Jesus Christ!*' Ox-Jo cursed as they stared down at the Lieutenant, lying huddled on the ledge, breathing harshly through his gaping mouth, his right leg doubled under him at an impossible angle.

'Hold your shit!' Jap snapped, staring first at the ashen-face teenage officer and then at the Tommies much further down the rockface. He made a quick calculation. It might take the British about ten minutes to reach the Lieutenant. By that time – with a bit of luck – they could have got him over the edge of the summit and hidden him somewhere in the shadows. 'Ox, give me covering fire. I'm going down.'

'Right.' Ox-Jo, his broad face unusually grim as he took in the young officer's pain-racked features and that unnaturally twisted leg, pulled out his automatic. He took careful aim and pulled the trigger. One of the Tommies flung up his arms wildly and started rolling down the hillside.

Jap utilized the diversion. He stood upright and dropped neatly onto the ledge next to the boy. Sepplmayr lay in a twisted heap, his face and hands bleeding furiously, but still conscious. 'Leave me,' he whispered through gritted teeth.

Jap said nothing. Instead he drew out his curved, razor-sharp Hunza knife. With his free hand, he grasped the boy's leg. Sepplmayr moaned with agony. Jap grunted an apology and with one sweep of his hand slit the grey cloth of the trouser-leg.

'*Ach, thou holy shit!*' he exclaimed, as he saw the white bone protruding through the red gore and swollen purple flesh. He had a compound fracture. With his leg in that state, Sepplmayr would barely be able to crawl.

'Is it . . . bad?' Sepplmayr asked through tightly clenched teeth. Jap didn't answer. Instead he said : 'We'll try to get up to the summit, sir.'

'I asked you a question, Corporal?'

'Yes, sir. Looks like a compound fracture to me. But all the same—'

'Leave me!' Sepplemayr said, iron in his voice.

'But sir!'

'There are no buts. You know the Colonel's orders?'

'But I can't just leave you here like that sir,' Jap protested wildly.

Sepplmayr raised his head painfully and his eyes full of horror stared at his ruined leg. 'I'd be lucky if I could go twenty metres with a leg like that,' he said. 'You can tell the C.O. I ordered you to leave me, Corporal.'

'But what will you do, sir?'

'Well, you can tell the Colonel, I didn't surrender to the Tommies, if that's what you mean, Corporal. I've still got my pistol. Now,' he swallowed hard, wanting to cry and beg the other man not to leave him to die here alone, 'you must go.'

'But sir,' Jap cried desperately, ducking as a slug hit the rock just above his contorted face.

Sepplmayr cursed in the thick accents of their native Bavaria. 'Will you go now, or am I to be forced to put a bullet through you for insubordination, Corporal!'

'All right, sir.' Jap took one last desperate look at the boy's ashen but determined face. Then he was gone, shinning up the rock face, drawing all the enemy fire onto himself.

Above him they had gone now, disappeared into the ever-growing shadows. Down below the British had not started moving again. Obviously they suspected a trap. Perhaps they thought the Germans were waiting for them to come over the top before opening fire.

Sepplmayr licked his cracked lips and looked at the big pistol which seemed to dwarf his thin hand. He clicked off the safety and opening his mouth, thrust the muzzle in between his lips. It was icy cold and tasted of oil. He gulped, both with nausea and fear.

Heinz Sepplmayr had always been afraid: afraid of his

96

father; of the rough peasant boys with whom he had played on holiday in the mountains; of the Hitler Youth leaders when his father had forced him to join the 'Movement of National Renewal'; of his all-knowing professors at the University; of the mountains and his superiors in Storm-troop Edelweiss. Fear had been his constant companion ever since he could remember. But now suddenly, for the first time in his young life, he was no longer afraid – just lonely and sad that it was all to end like this before it had really started. He had never even 'had' a woman!

He pulled himself together suddenly. Even if he shot himself the Tommies would still find his body and be able to identify his unit from his typical Alpine Corps equipment. *He couldn't die here!*

With a supreme effort of will, he reached forward and grasped the nearest handhold. The pain in his crippled leg was excruciating. He bit his bottom lip and heaved. Trying not to alarm the Tommies below, he inched his way forward, heading for where the hill overlooked the sea.

In the haze that wavered, cleared and then threatened to swamp him, he could just make out the edge of the hill and beyond the dark-green, sombre stretch of Aegean. He was nearly there now.

'Halt – or I'll shoot!' a voice commanded.

His vaguely-remembered school English told him the words meant danger. But he did not care. He was too far gone to worry about such things now. He crawled, dragging his right leg after him.

'Halt!'

The roar of the sea was overpowering now. Even at that height he felt its salty tang assailing his nostrils.

He dragged himself up to his full height, his bloody hands no longer feeling the pain of the sharp rocks slicing into them. Bullets whined off the stone all around him. Below, far below, the sea swayed wildly back and forth, exercising an hypnotic fascination upon him.

Leutnant der Reserve Heinz Sepplmayr drew one last breath. 'I'm coming!' he cried fervently as he launched himself forward at that same instant that the Irish Fusilier officer's last shot struck the side of his cap and knocked it off his head. A moment later he had disappeared beneath the waves a hundred metres below.

His peaked cap with the *Edelweiss* badge lay on the rocky ground behind him. Sepplmayr was accident-prone right to the very end!

SEVEN

'My God, Charley,' Colonel French said to the bedraggled captain, 'you look as if you've been dragged through a hedge backwards! What in heaven's name happened to you and the patrol?'

Captain O'Kane of 'B' Company, the Irish Fusiliers, ducked as yet another German bomb exploded a couple of hundred yards away from the Battalion HQ and waited until the noise had subsided before he answered. 'We bumped into something or other. I don't know exactly what but they led us a devil of a dance.'

Swiftly the captain explained how his patrol had flushed out three men who had led them into the hills near the coast, where two of them had vanished in the darkness while the other one, obviously badly wounded, had committed suicide by flinging himself over the cliff.

French took his pipe from his mouth with a steady hand. 'My God,' he exclaimed, 'what absolute fanaticism! But what were they? Local wog, or Jerry?'

'Don't know exactly. In that light and at that distance, we couldn't make out whether they were wearing uniform or civvies, sir. But we did find this. It looks Jerry to me, sir.' The captain pulled Sepplmayr's cap out of his pocket and dropped it on the packing-case table.

Colonel French picked it up curiously. 'Obviously German,' he said, turning the grey peaked cap around in his hands. 'But what's this?'

'It's some sort of badge, sir. Looks like a flower.'

French held the metal badge up to the flickering light of the candle. 'You know what your flower is, Charley?' he said after a moment.

'No sir.'

'Well, if I'm not very mistaken, it's an Edelweiss.'

'And what's that mean sir?'

'It's the badge of the German mountain troops. Those chaps you were chasing were Jerry mountaineers!'

'But what are they up to on Leros?'

By way of answer, Colonel French got to his feet and taking up the candle, walked over to the map tacked to the wall of the bunker. 'The Fortress is out,' he said, as if he were talking to himself. 'It's not in our sector and the Jerries you spotted were definitely in Irish Fusilier territory.'

'Right, sir,' the Captain agreed, wondering what the 'Old Man' was getting at.

Colonel French ran his forefinger along the line of the Rachi Ridge thoughtfully. 'Rachi perhaps. No, I think the Ridge is out. It has little tactical advantage as long as we hold the Fortress on Mount Neraviglia.' He sucked his front teeth and made his decision. 'Mount Clidi – it has to be Mount Clidi!'

'I don't follow you, sir,' the captain said.

Colonel French spun round on him, 'Charley, what have the Eyeties got up on the top of Clidi?'

'Just their artillery.'

'No infantry?'

'No sir, apart from a couple of mule skinners who bring up their supplies, if you can class them as infantry.'

'Balls!' French cursed. 'Don't you see, Charley? Those Eyeties up there are the only people capable of stopping an airborne landing on the northern part of the island.'

'But intelligence—'

'Intelligence can go and take a running jump! I put my money on the Jerries trying an airborne landing on Leros. They did it at Crete, I don't see why they shouldn't try the same tactic on Leros.' He waved his hand irritably at the younger officer. 'Now Charley, what's the state of your "B" Company?'

'Pretty buggered, sir. Half the chaps were with me on that sweep this afternoon and the rest were manning the ack-ack, such as it is. My guess is that most of the chaps haven't had a good night's sleep for over a week now.'

Colonel French looked grim. 'Well, I'm afraid they're just going to have to forego it for yet another night. It's my guess that tonight the Jerry will have a crack at Clidi and when he does I want "B" Company, the Royal Irish Fusiliers, waiting for him up there to give him a nice, warm welcome . . .'

EIGHT

Just before they began the ascent, Colonel Stuermer had run over the old textbook formula for a new climb 'T$=$A + P + E.' It signified that a climber should not select the target – 'T' – before he had assessed 'A', the ability of the climbing team. Well, there had been no problem there. 'P', the prevailing conditions, was a different matter. They were lousy: a new slope, obviously thought insurmountable by the Italians, for they had no guards on it, to be ascended in pitch darkness. 'E' – equipment – was the same. Back at their base they had equipment enough, but under the conditions prevailing on Clidi they could use only the bare essentials; there would be no time for elaborate kit. He had concluded that, according to the textbook formula, Stormtroop Edelweiss should not even go near Mount Clidi.

But in spite of his misgivings, the early stages of the ascent had been surprisingly easy. Since the recce photo of the mountain had been taken, there had been a heavy fall of boulders. Although they had been forced by the darkness to take it slowly, they had scrambled over the fallen boulders without too much difficulty.

But now, just as Meier and Corporal Madad returned to report that Sepplmayr had killed himself, the full difficulty of their night ascent became apparent. Above Stuermer there towered what appeared to be a sheer precipice, barely visible and obviously a tough nut to crack.

'What do you think, Colonel?' Greul whispered. 'Should we attempt to traverse to the right? Perhaps it might be easier over there.'

'Possibly, Greul, but I don't think we have the time.'

'You mean because of Sepplmayr?'

'Yes. If they can get down the cliff and recover his body – well,' Colonel Stuermer left the rest of the sentence unfinished.

'They might guess what we mountain troops are after?'

'Yes, even if they think a three man party is just a recce force, checking the route for a later invasion party. No, we've got to get up this thing by the quickest route possible.'

'Right you are, sir,' Greul said without hesitation. The Major might be an arrogant, ruthless bastard, but he was a fine climber and definitely no coward.

'All right, Greul, I'll go first.' Stuermer stared up at what appeared to be the rock chimney, its shadowy mouth just a blurred rectangle against the night sky. He took the rope from his shoulder and said, 'We'll rope up and tell the men to do the same. I'm not going to attempt to look for the crack in this murk. We'll use the ropes to get as far as the chimney. Clear?'

'Clear,' Greul snapped back in his super-efficient manner and passed the order to rope up to the man following him.

'And Greul, any spikes we use, we'll work in by hand.'

'*Jawohl, Herr Oberst!*'

Colonel Stuermer uncoiled the kernmantel rope and felt for the first handhold. The ascent of Mount Clidi had begun!

'Come on, you shower of broken-down Belfast layabouts!' Captain Charley O'Kane cried in the best Irish accent he could muster. In spite of his Irish name, the O'Kanes had been pure Home Counties for the best part of two centuries. 'Remember we've got to get to the top before the Jerries. Remember the Battle of the Boyne!' he added cheerfully and nearly sprawled full length when his foot went into a pot-hole in the inky darkness.

For the last hour they had chased across the rugged countryside. In spite of his men's tiredness, he had forced them into a speed march – run five minutes, march five – until he had had them gasping leathern-lunged and swaying like drunken men. But he had allowed no respite. They *had* to make that summit before the Jerries!

Now he was forced to slow down. The track was too steep and winding, made treacherous by the pot-holes everywhere. He knew his Irishmen were all right, as long as they had a leader; they were bold, aggressive soldiers. But without a leader they went to pieces, incapable of making decisions. He had to look after himself.

Wrinkling his nose at the stench of mule droppings and panting with the effort of the climb, O'Kane stared upwards. He could vaguely make out the summit. He glanced at the green glowing dial of his wrist-watch.

Nearly midnight. If what the Old Man suspected was correct, the Jerries would already be attempting to climb Mount Clidi and there was no sign of an Eyetie sentry anywhere. 'Come on, me lucky lads!' he called, but there was no warmth, only anxiety in his young voice, 'let's be having yer. We don't want to be too late for the party, do we?'

Slowly Stuermer felt the rock face for a hold. Behind him he could hear the laboured breathing of his men as they worked their way up the route he had found for them. His bleeding fingers bumped into something. He touched it carefully. A jug handle! He beamed in the darkness. It was one of the best handholds, over which all five fingers could curl and from which the climber could hang out to improve foot friction. With infinite care, he eased a spike

102

from his belt and using as much force as he dared, began working it into the rock at waist-level. With that in position and the jug-handle above, the men following would have little difficulty passing this particular spot.

His task finished, Stuermer rested for a moment. He knew that time was precious, but all the same one could not rush a climb of this kind. *'Eile mit Weile'** had to be their motto this particular night.

The beginning of the chimney was twenty metres away now. Perhaps a matter of ten minutes before he reached it. He took a deep breath, feeling no fear and no tiredness, just a sense of elation. Once again he was in his element, facing the challenge of the mountains against which all the bloody challenges of war palled.

'I'm moving on, Greul,' he called softly. 'And pass it on – as quietly as possible now.'

Playing out the rope a little more so that it acted as a guide for the men following, he reached upwards once more. Five minutes passed. Ten. He worked his way steadily up the face of the rock. It was difficult, but not impossible. Now he was almost within grasping distance of the entrance to the chimney. Thereafter they would be able to dispense with equipment and move more rapidly. He reached up, feeling for a handhold. Suddenly the tiny outcrop on which he was balanced gave!

Stuermer caught his cry of alarm just in time as he began to slide in a shower of rock. But one of Europe's greatest climbers was not destined to die on Mount Clidi that night. A sudden blow to his stomach made him gasp violently and then he had stopped. His belt buckle had caught in the last spike he had driven in the rock!

'You all right?' Greul's voice asked anxiously from below.

Stuermer swallowed hard. 'Yes . . . Just indulging in a few games with myself.'

'Can I help?'

'No, I'll cope.' Stuermer allowed himself to hang there for a few moments, till he had overcome the shock of the

*Virtually untranslatable. Roughly, 'hurry at leisure.'

103

fall, getting his breath back and assessing his situation. Although the spike was supporting his whole weight, he reckoned it would hold him for at least a couple of minutes. He cast around in the darkness for a hold but could see nothing. Gingerly he reached upwards, feeling the spike at his waist move frighteningly. He took a chance and straining his body upwards, in spite of the ominous creak of the steadily loosening spike, felt the rock higher up. Nothing! Now he was afraid. Time was running out rapidly. Behind him the whole column had come to a stop, waiting tensely for the outcome of this silent battle between man and nature.

Stuermer knew he must take one final chance. Placing his right hand flat against the rock face so that it gave him a little support, smoothed his left hand outwards. Slowly, as slowly as he dared, he ran it downwards, the sweat pouring from his body. Then he had it. A vertical crack about half a metre away! His heart leapt with relief. It didn't feel any bigger than a matchstick, but it would be sufficient to give him leverage upwards. Saying a rapid prayer that the spike would not give before he positioned himself for the jump upwards, he crooked his fingers into the crack. He would use it as a sidepull hold. The whole of his weight was still supported by the buckle, but in a moment he would transfer it to the sidepull hold. He took a deep breath and, just as the spike finally gave clattering noisily down the slope before pitching right over the precipice, he threw his whole weight onto the tiny hold. He had done it!

Five minutes later, his hands bleeding badly from a myriad small cuts, his knees badly bruised, ashen-faced and panting, but with a grin of triumph on his face, Stuermer was packed into the bottom of the chimney, ready to begin the last stage of that terrible night climb.

'Christ, sir,' a Fusilier gasped, 'do dem donkeys really climb dis track?'

O'Kane, bent almost double like the rest of the exhausted men strung out in single file behind him, swallowed and panted. 'Yes, Collins . . . they don't just climb . . . they're double up it . . .'

'Sweet Jasus, I don't believe it!'

'Bash on, lads. Remember the old Fusilier spirit,' O'Kane gasped. 'There'll be a jar on me . . . for everyone of you . . . if we beat Jerry to the top.'

Out to sea the darkness was broken by scarlet stabs of flame coming from plane exhausts and to the south in the direction of the Fortress the gongs were beginning to clang, wafted miles across the silent countryside by the night wind. O'Kane knew what that meant. The Jerries were coming in for yet another raid. He glanced up at the summit of the mountain. As yet it was as silent as ever. Not a sentry in sight. But surely the alarm would wake them. Even the Eyetie Army stood to in an air-raid.

Then he concentrated on the backbreaking task of climbing the treacherous track. Now it would be only a matter of minutes and they would be there. In spite of his exhaustion and the strain, O'Kane smiled in the darkness. The Irish had done it. They had definitely beaten the Jerries to the top.

The roar of many engines from the sea grew ever louder. Leros was in for a full-scale raid again that night.

Stuermer's muscles were ablaze with agony. His breath rasped in harsh gulping gasps in and out of his starved lungs. Yet he forced himself upwards, using the classic back and foot technique of climbing the chimney.

It was a murderous effort, but his objective was within sight. Some ten or fifteen metres above his head, there was a patch of dark sky, which signified they were nearly at the summit. Deliberately Stuermer dismissed the pain from his consciousness, listening to the ever-increasing roar of the approaching planes.

In spite of the brutal pain, which tortured his body, he was pleased and proud of himself and his men. They were among the handful of men in the whole world who could have carried off such a task : to climb an unknown mountain in pitch darkness, laden with fighting gear and using only the minimum of equipment. Noiselessly he pulled himself over the top and lay there gasping, the roar of the bombers almost on top of him now. He could just make out the long barrels of the Italian guns and the little two-man tents. But despite the roar in the sky above, the Italian gunners slept on.

'Typical spaghetti-eaters,' Greul said contemptuously as he pulled himself over the edge of the chimney and flopped next to Stuermer, who noted that the young officer was hardly breathing hard. 'Absolutly no security whatsoever.'

'Be grateful that our ex-allies like their sacks,' Stuermer answered, trying to control his hectic breathing. 'Be—' He stopped short.

A dark figure had appeared just beyond the guns. A voice shouted something in English and was answered by frightened cries in Italian. The next moment a red flare had hissed into the night sky and suddenly they were frozen and exposed in its blood red light. *They had been spotted!*

NINE

'*Flare!*' the gunner bellowed over the intercom. '*Flare to port, captain!*'

The pilot of the leading Stuka turned his head and peered down quickly.

A red light had broken the inky blackness. He screwed up his eyes. He wasn't certain, but he thought he could just make out the spiked silhouette of the mountain HQ they had been looking for for the last ten minutes. He glanced at the fuel warning light. It hadn't begun to flash yet, but he was nearly on reserve.

'What do you think, captain?' the gunner's voice crackled metallicly over the intercom.

The Commander of the Third Stuka Wing hesitated. His orders from Mueller had been to bomb Mount Meraviglia

106

to cover the dawn airborne drop. But was this Meraviglia or Clidi, which might well be in German hands by now?

The flickering light on the panel, which indicated that his fuel was down to exactly five minutes flying time, made up his mind for him. He pressed his throat mike and switched over to the command channel. 'Red leader to red attack force. Going into the attack now! Over and out!'

The Stuka pilot thrust forward the controls. The gull-winged dive-bomber dropped alarmingly to port. Behind him the other pilots, eyes fixed on his twin exhaust flames, prepared to do the same.

'Hold on gunner – here we go!' the pilot screamed, sensing that old, old exhilaration.

Next instant the dive bomber fell out of the sky, screaming down directly for the spot where the flare was extinguishing itself, its sirens going with a hellish banshee howl.

'*Stukas!*' O'Kane yelled furiously above the sudden racket. 'Down everyone!'

The Fusiliers forgot their tiredness. As one they flung themselves on the track.

O'Kane kept his face pressed down tight, as the first plane, its noise filling the whole world, hurtled out of the sky. Surely it must plummet straight into the ground! When it seemed that nothing could prevent it smashing into the mountainside, the plane's pilot pulled it out of the tremendous dive.

Bombs by the score came wobbling out of the Stuka's belly. O'Kane chanced a look upwards, as the sky filled with them. '*Incendiaries!*' he screamed. The first plane's job was either to light up the area for the rest of the flight, or to set alight the scrub with which the hillside was covered.

As the next plane came hurtling in, the little fire bombs plopped and began to explode everywhere. In an instant the mountainside was alight, as the hissing magnesium splattered out and set the trees afire.

'Back . . . back!' Captain O'Kane cried hysterically, springing to his feet, his figure outlined black against the glaring incandescent whiteness. 'For Chrissake . . . move back!'

His Fusiliers needed no urging. They fell back hastily, as the first HE* began whistling down on their positions, scrambling down the mountainside to avoid that frightening wall of fire, leaving the Italians to their fate.

The first wild shot to their rear alerted the Italian artillerymen to the ambush. Half-naked gunners ran wildly back and forth, trying to find some way out of the trap in which they found themselves, while furious officers, buckling on their equipment, screamed contradictory orders at them. Now gunners started to fall everywhere as the enemy began to take more careful aim. The sight of the dead and the knowledge that there was no way through the roaring wall of flame to their rear had a steadying effect on the Italians. Under the command of a grey-haired captain, his shoulder bleeding heavily from a burst of Schmeisser fire, they backed towards their outdated guns, firing and giving ground, stopping, firing and giving ground again.

Greul, at the head of the Edelweiss men coming in on the left flank, yelled above the crackle of small arms fire, 'Don't let them solidify! Keep at them!'

Now the surviving Italians were silhouetted against the blazing scrub to their rear, almost impossible targets to miss. Man after man crumpled and dropped to the ground. Now the Italians were backing up against the red wall of fire, which was only twenty or thirty yards from their ancient cannon.

Stuermer saw the danger. Once they reached the metal shields of the cannon, they would be safe from the Edelweiss troopers' light calibre weapons. Their courage would return. They would realize they were armed with 76mm cannon against which the enemy only had hand-fire weapons. They would resist and pin the mountain men

*High explosive.

108

down, and as soon as the flames had subsided the English infantry would return and stiffen the Italian defence.

'Cut them off from those damned guns!' he yelled at the top of his voice, 'use your grenades.' A missile exploded behind the wounded Italian officer. He staggered violently, but remained on his feet. Taking deliberate aim with his pistol, one hand behind his back as if he were firing on some peacetime range, he fired. Next to Stuermer a trooper clapped his hand to his shoulder and yelped with pain. Stuermer caught his potato masher just before he dropped it from his suddenly nerveless fingers. With the four second fuse spluttering furiously, he flung it at the lone officer.

It exploded directly in front of him in a flash of angry violent flame. The officer seemed to fly backwards as if struck dead by some gigantic fist.

Suddenly the heart went out of the Italians. Everywhere survivors began to toss away their weapons and raise their hands, crying in broken German: *'Nix schiessen, . . . nix schiessen, tedeschi!'*

The victorious troopers surged forward. Swiftly the middle-aged Italians were disarmed and frisked. Colonel Stuermer doubled forward, springing over the bodies of the dead, and stopping at the first gun. In a flash he had whipped out the firing mechanism. With one swift blow he broke the exposed firing pin against a rock; and the next; and yet another.

Stuermer completed his task and leaning against the last of the now useless cannon breathed out hard. They had done it in spite of everything. Their journey of two thousand kilometres had paid dividends. *Mount Glidi was firmly in German hands!*

Part Four

THE END IN LEROS

ONE

On the top of the mountain they waited. Soon it would be dawn and then the Tommies, creatures of habit, would attack. All that night they and their Italian prisoners had dug in feverishly, preparing the mountain-top position for the counter-attack that must come.

In the command dug-out, Stuermer and Greul talked in that subdued, slow manner of men at night, discussing other places and other times, remote from the war-torn landscape all around them. 'The problems in the Himalayas, Greul, are different from those of the Alps. In the Alps you have to make supreme mental and physical effort for a few days at the most. The Himalayas demand more from a climber. That kind of strain has to be endured for weeks, perhaps even months, before one can attempt the final all-out thrust to the top. And how often are the climbers worn out by what has gone before when it comes to that final ascent; they fail and pay the full penalty for that failure. Think of our beloved German Mountain*?'

'Nanga Parbat?'

'Yes.'

'Yes, it has taken its toll of our comrades, Colonel,' Greul said softly. 'Merkl and Willo Welzenbach in '34. In '37, it took seven of our best climbers.' His voice hardened. 'But one has to pay the price for failure in blood. The New Germany tolerates no failure. There can only be victory or death!'

'Can there?' Stuermer queried. He stared up at the fading stars. They had shone for countless lifetimes before he had been born and they would continue to do so for many lifetimes after he was dead. They would remain

*Nanga Parbat in Kashmir, 26,620 ft high, was the special preserve of German climbers until it was finally climbed by Hermann Buhl in 1953.

unaffected whether he and his men died this new day, or whether he survived to have one last crack at the great mountain in the far-off Himalayas. *Victory or death!* What did that matter in the great scheme of things?

In the next foxhole, Jap and Ox-Jo chatted quietly too, their machine-pistols propped up against the earth walls. 'How did you come to join up, Ox?' Jap enquired, chewing on a looted Italian salami sausage.

'I volunteered.'

'The only place you'd volunteer for would be bouncer at a Munich knocking shop.'

'It's true, you consumptive bastard,' Ox-Jo persisted, 'Well almost. I was in a cafe in Schwabing.'

'*Boozer* you mean!'

'Well, boozer. Opposite me a Prussian. I stare, he stares back. A beermat flies through the air. The Prussian gets a toothpick stuck up his snout. Mrs Meier's handsome boy a tube of mustard squeezed into his ear. A bottle of beer gets smashed over the Prussian's head and suddenly out of the blue there's trouble and the police are there—'

But Jap was never fated to hear how his comrade had been forced into the army, for at that precise moment the dawn sky was torn apart by the grunt and howl of the first British mortar bomb.

'Incoming mail!' Jap yelled.

'Here we go again,' Ox-Jo growled, grabbing his machine-pistol, as the mortar barrage cascaded upon the German positions.

'First platoon ready to move, sir!'

'Second platoon ready to move, sir!'

'Third platoon . . .'

All along the line the gruff shouts came ringing back to where O'Kane stood next to chattering radio, strapped on the back of the radioman.

O'Kane looked at his wrist watch. Five minutes to go. All around him the hundred odd survivors of 'B' Company were formed up, ready to go. Old hands that they were;

they did not seem to notice the frenzied roar of the support company's mortars and the amplified staccato of the shell bursts up above. Instead they performed mundane tasks like tying up their boot laces, adjusting their battle packs, urinating on the charred grass, without the rhythm of their actions being disturbed at all.

O'Kane nodded his approval. When it came to the prospect of a scrap, their Irish blood made them the best fighters in the world. He reached for the mike and clicked the switch to 'send': 'Hello Sunray . . . Hello Sunray. Two here . . . Hello Sunray . . .'

'Sunray here.' Colonel French's voice came through loud and clear. 'What is it Two?'

'All ready, Sunray.'

'Excellent, Two . . . One and Three' – Colonel French meant the Battalion's 'A' and 'C' companies – 'in position too. Give it five more and then push off, Two.'

'Understood, Sunray. Five more to go. Over.'

'Good luck, Two.'

'Thank you, sir.' O'Kane flushed. He had dropped a clanger!

At the other end, Colonel French chuckled sympathetically. 'I know, I know, Two. I'm sure the other chap' – he meant the enemy – 'has known our call signs for the last three years. Over and out!'

As the sky started to flush the faint pink of the new day, Captain O'Kane ran over the Irish Fusiliers' plan of attack. 'B' Company would kick off the attack with a frontal assault on the German positions. Five minutes after they had gone in, 'A' would attack on the left flank and 'C' on the right. The idea was that 'B' would draw the enemy fire, while 'A' and 'C' would catch the Jerries on the hop. O'Kane bit his lip. 'B' had got the dirty end of the stick again, but his Paddies didn't seem to mind. They were itching for a fight.

He looked at the glowing hands of his watch. It was nearly time to go. Above, the controlled cyclone of mortar fire was subsiding. He would attack one minute before it was due to end so he would catch the Jerries with their heads still down.

'Four . . . three . . .' he counted off the minutes aloud . . . 'two.' He blew three shrill blasts on his whistle. '*MOVE OUT – "B"!*' he bellowed over the crump of the exploding mortar bombs. '*AT THE DOUBLE NOW, LADS!*'

'*ACHTUNG! . . . DIE TOMMIES KOMMEN!*' an urgent voice cried, as the barrage began to die away.

'*STAND TO EVERYWHERE*', Colonel Stuermer cried. '*HERE THEY COME!*'

A frenzy of fumbling – that instant of panic before they had sighted their weapons – the Tommy grenades exploding everywhere on the summit as they came screaming and yelling up the battle-littered slope, bayonets fixed. Ox-Jo took his time. As the smoke of the shelling cleared, he spotted the target he was looking for : a Tommy with the three white stripes of a sergeant on his khaki sleeve. He crooked his finger around the Schmeisser's trigger and squeezed it gently. The machine-pistol hissed venemously.

Ox-Jo could see the lumps of flesh flying from the Tommy's body. What looked like a line of red buttonholes appearing on the front of his shirt. Still he kept on coming. 'God in heaven !' Ox-Jo cried angrily. 'Will you never go down, you Tommy bastard !' He emptied a full burst into the man at twenty metres' range. The sergeant disappeared in a welter of flying blood and massacred flesh.

Now the Tommies were going down everywhere. The morning air was full of blood-chilling screams for 'stretcher-bearers.' Still the Tommies did not break. They were only ten metres from the Stormtroop's position now. Carried away by a savage blood-lust, Ox-Jo and Jap leapt out of their foxholes and standing completely exposed on the parapet, fired burst after burst into the advancing Tommies, swinging their Schmeissers from the hip, hosing them down in unthinking cruelty.

Suddenly, when it seemed the Irish must swamp the German positions, they broke. With the same speed and

116

frenzy with which they had attacked, they swung round and went streaming down the body-littered slope.

But there was no respite for the mountaineers. As 'B' Company broke, 'A' and 'C' companies hit the German flanks.

Colonel Stuermer reacted instinctively. Bending down, he pushed away the dead gunner lying over the Spandau next to him. Not noticing the searingly hot barrel, he cradled it in his bare arms, two belts of ammunition slung around his neck, and ran to the hard pressed right flank.

Already the first English had hit the German positions. All along the perimeter, mountaineers and Tommies were locked together in hand-to-hand combat. When a man went down, no quarter was given. The victor savagely stamped the fallen man into the earth with his iron-shod boots.

Stuermer knew his men on the perimeter could deal with the Tommies who had managed to penetrate their line. It was those who were following who worried him. Smashing a path for himself through the struggling mass with the butt of the Spandau, he flung himself into a hole behind them and faced down the slope. The second wave of Tommy infantry were coming in now, crying in hoarse triumph, knowing that the absence of fire meant their comrades had knocked out the first German line.

Stuermer rammed the wooden butt into his right shoulder. He fed the first belt into the slot and jerked back the trigger. Vicious scarlet flame jetted from the gun's muzzle. Bullets at the rate of eight hundred a minute hit the English line.

The Tommies stopped as if they had hit a brick wall. For a moment the survivors stood there stupidly, as if they didn't know what to do. Stuermer pressed the trigger once more. Tracer zipped through the air furiously and slugs struck them, whirling them round and smashing them to the ground like broken dolls.

It was more than they could stand. Just as Greul's green flare soared into the dawn sky to indicate that he had thrown back the attack on the left flank, the Tommies broke completely. Streaming down the slope, they fled.

Stuermer slumped over the machine-gun and gulped in air, noting for the first time the stench of burning flesh. He looked down. The red-hot barrel of the Spandau had raised a blister extending from his singed shirt-sleeve all the way to his fingers.

But there was no time to worry about his burn now. For as the last of the attackers disappeared behind the cover of the boulders, the British mortars opened up once again.

The veterans of Stormtroop Edelweiss, hardened on every front from Narvik in the far north to the Caucasus in the far south, knew what to expect.

At once paralysis descended upon the mountaineers' positions. All firing stopped. The mountaineers huddled in fearful expectancy in their pits, their heads pressed against the sweating backs of the men next to them. The roar grew in intensity. Drowning out all other sound, the world consisted solely of that hoarse exultant scream. With a great earth-shaking crash, one hundred mortar bombs hit the summit.

All hell was let loose. Purple flame ripped the grey dawn apart. Red-hot slices of razor-sharp shrapnel slashed through the air. Showers of earth and rock shot upwards. Suddenly the dawn was alive with the agonized cries of wounded and mangled men.

Stuermer groaned in misery and risked a look upwards. 'Where are the paras?' he asked aloud. 'Where?'

But the dawn sky, blood-red now with exploding shells, remained blank and empty.

TWO

'*Leros, Herr Baron*,' the pilot cried from the cockpit of the three-engined Junkers transport.

Baron von Waldstein, Commander of the Fourth Parachute Battalion, the 'Green Devils', pushed his way down the corridor between his tense paras. Peering over the pilot's shoulder, his monocle jammed firmly in his right eye, he stared down at the little brown smudge of land set in the deep green of the dawn sea.

'Hairy,' he pronounced.

'Definitely, Baron,' the pilot, a cheerful lieutenant, agreed. 'Land on one of those mountains and you'll get a nasty pain in your arse!'

Von Waldstein craned his head around. Through the glinting perspex of the cockpit, he could see that the rest of the 'Auntie Jus', as the Green Devils called the ancient transport planes, were in perfect formation. They were flying in an extended V, dragging enormous black shadows across the still surface of the Aegean. He turned his attention to the peaks of the Rachi Ridge over which he and his five hundred men would have to jump.

It was going to be tricky. An opposed jump over mountains was bad enough, but on an island as small as Leros, his Green Devils could easily be swept out to sea as the British paras had been at Sicily. 'What's the wind speed, Lieutenant?'

'Must be all of thirty knots, Baron.'

'How jolly for us,' von Waldstein said. 'Give my chaps something to think about instead of idling their time away while they're coming down. All right, Lieutenant, we might as well get the nasty business over with. Fancy having to throw oneself out of an aeroplane at this time of the morning? Definitely not on.'

Baron von Waldstein stamped back into the fuselage. He nodded to the sergeant dispatcher, who looked as pale and as apprehensive as the Green Devils, and positioned himself at the open door, the wind whipping at his baggy jump overalls. He would be the first out of the first stick. As he was fond of saying to his officers in the mess, 'A chap likes to get off first, doesn't he? Keeps him from having to mix with the common folk.'

119

The Junkers were now passing over the coast. Erratic fire was beginning to come up, exploding in sudden cotton-wool puffs of smoke, rocking the planes. The Baron did not even notice. His monocled gaze was fixed on the peaks of the Rachi Ridge. Behind him the paras were singing their song:

'When Germany is in danger, there is only one way for us.
To fight and to conquer. To accept we must die.
From our planes, my friend, there is no return.'

They were down to four hundred and fifty metres now. The pilot was bringing the Junkers down rapidly. At one hundred and fifty he would level out and they would jump. It was pretty low. By jumping at that height, they risked injured backs and broken limbs. Still they stood a better chance of not being whipped away by the wind and their time of descent would be reduced drastically, giving the Tommies less chance to 'put one up the spout', as his Green Devils called their most feared wound – a bullet in the groin.

'*Fertig!*' von Waldstein called. They were almost over the dropping zone. 'One minute to go.' He tensed and gave his equipment one last check.

Opposite him the red light began to wink urgently. They were over the DZ.

The Baron did not wait for the signal to jump. Taking a deep breath, he launched himself into space. The weight of his pack and battle equipment seemed to snatch him out of the plane. He started to hurtle downwards at a terrifying rate. Crack! The ripcord snapped. A great white mushroom of silk billowed open above him.

He said his habitual prayer and then he was fighting the wind, ignoring the red tracer winging its way like a swarm of angry bees.

To his horror, he saw that the wind was beginning to sweep him out to sea. And he was not the only one. All around, his Green Devils were struggling frantically with

120

their shroud lines, fighting against the wind. The gleaming sea loomed closer and closer. He could see the white line of the breakers coming up on his left.

Then he had it. The 'chute was emptying of air. He was descending much faster now. Tiny figures were running towards him up a steep slope. Whether they were German or British, he did not know, nor did he care at that moment. His main concern was not breaking a limb.

He tensed. Instinctively he drew up his knees to protect himself better, as a patch of pine wood rushed up to meet him.

He hit it at 50 kilometres an hour. Twigs ripped his face. His nostrils were assailed by the heavy odour of pine as he crashed through the trees. A branch snapped back and struck him across the face. He blacked out momentarily. He came to just as his boots hit the ground with an impact that seemed to send his legs thrusting into his stomach. He just had enough strength to hit the quick-release catch at his belly and free the 'chute. It blew away with the next gust of wind, leaving him there, gasping for breath furiously.

Far away he could hear faint shouts. He knew he could not risk them belonging to Englishmen. He scrambled to his feet and looked around. No one in sight. He unslung his machine-pistol and pulling out his monocle, inserted it firmly into his eye. Feeling a little better now, but limping badly, Baron von Waldstein set out to find his missing Green Devils . . .

'Impossible!' Colonel Tilney had exploded at the Fortress HQ when a runner had brought in the news that the Germans were landing paratroops over the Rachi Ridge.

'But they are, sir,' the runner protested. 'I saw them myself. Hundreds o' them. A lot of the buggers going straight into the drink.'

Tilney recovered quickly enough. There were no men to spare from defensive duties so in the end he sent out a scratch force of cooks and clerks, batmen and drivers to round the Germans up.

They had an easy task. It was sheer slaughter. The mixed bag of headquarters staffmen massacred the German paras, caught in the trees by their shrouded lines or sprawled helplessly up to their waists in water, burdened by their water-logged canopies.

Many of them hung dead in the harnesses, their 'chutes filling and deflating with the changing wind like enormous silken lungs. Only here and there lay a discarded overall, abandoned like the shell of some strange insect, indicating that its owner had managed to escape.

By ten o'clock that morning, von Waldstein had managed to collect a hundred of his Green Devils. For a while they had been pinned down in a maize field at the edge of the Ridge, which was their objective. In the end the Baron had grown desperate.

Shouting, 'We have not been sent to Leros to lie in a field having our arses toasted by the Aegean sun!' he had sprung to his feet and followed by a handful of the braver of his men, he had charged the British, firing from the hip as he ran. His suicidal attack had caught the Tommies by surprise. The motley force of cooks and clerks fell back. In a flash the paras were through them and doubling strenuously uphill towards the heights, leaving half a dozen dead behind them.

That had been thirty minutes earlier. Now the survivors – perhaps eighty men in all – were marching steadily towards their objective, the only sound that of their harsh breathing and the renewed rumble of artillery on Mount Clidi to their right. In spite of their disastrous drop, the Green Devils had almost cut off the north of the island from the centre. Now General Mueller's seaborne forces could begin their landings!

THREE

Colonel Maurice French was very angry. 'Tilney,' he snapped, 'they have done exactly what I said they would – drop paratroopers! Now they've got us over a barrel.'

'What do you mean?' Tilney barked, his face just as angry as French's.

'Well, look at the situation now. The paratroopers have pressed right across country. I know small parties of Jellicoe's people are giving them some trouble. But we can't blind ourselves to the fact that the Jerries are holding everywhere and that our people in the north are cut off. It won't be very long before Jerry sends in his seaborne force.'

'All right, French,' Tilney said, holding up his hand for peace. 'I'll admit you were right. But that is past history. The problem is what are we going to do about it, *now*?'

'Immediate counter-attacks,' French answered without the slightest hesitation, although he knew his own Paddies were exhausted.

'Where?'

'At two points. At Mount Clidi.'

'But you were forced to withdraw your Fusiliers from there when the paratroopers came down.'

'Agreed, Tilney. That job will be up to Colonel Iggulden's Buffs* in the north. I know that they'll be attacking from the wrong side of the Mount, but if the Jerries could scale it so can our people.'

'I don't know about that, but I'll get on the blower to Iggulden immediately we're finished here. Now what about the other spot where you think we should attack?'

'Tilney, I don't have to remind you that one of the first principles one learns at Staff College is not to allow one's forces to be spread about in penny packets. At this

*The Royal East Kent Regt.

moment it is vital that we concentrate so that we are able to hit the Jerries for six when they start their landings.'

'Agreed. So what are you suggesting, French?'

'An immediate counter-attack by my own Fusiliers on the paratroopers on Rachi Ridge. Break through them and link up with the Buffs, ready to attack wherever necessary with a two-battalion-strong force.'

Colonel Tilney never had a chance to reply. Suddenly the clatter of the field phone on his desk broke in. He picked it up and barked 'Tilney'. Impatiently waiting for him to finish, French saw how Tilney's face suddenly grew more and more pale. 'What is it?' he asked anxiously when Tilney had rammed the phone down on its cradle once more.

'Too late, French.'

'Too late for what, man?'

Tilney licked his suddenly dry lips and looked at French, all hope gone from his eyes. 'The Jerries have just begun landing troops at Parteni Bay in Buff territory.'

'Bloody hell!' Colonel French beat his clenched fist on the table in the gesture of a man who had been tried just too much.

Just as the keen-eyed Jap spotted the three green flares which indicated that the paras were in possession of the Rachi Ridge to their front and that their mission on Clidi was over, Greul barked urgently, 'Colonel Stuermer!'

Stuermer, his tired face wreathed in a smile, spun round. 'What is it, Greul?'

Greul pointed to their left. 'New troops,' he said, 'and there are more coming in on the other flank. Looks like two companies, perhaps five hundred men in all.'

'Yes,' Stuermer said grimly. 'Far too many for us to handle, especially when they're covered by those bren carriers. They're not much in the way of armour, but we've got no anti-tank weapons and those things can climb the frontal slope. Besides I don't want to waste another life on Clidi. The guns are spiked. It has no value to us anymore.'

124

'Agreed. We must link up with the paras. But what are we going to do, Colonel?'

'We've got to keep the Tommies at a safe distance till dark and then get away.'

'But how, sir?'

'I'll show you,' Stuermer cried. He bounded forward and threw himself into a forward foxhole next to a slightly wounded trooper. 'Give me your carbine,' he ordered.

Swiftly Stuermer dug into his pocket and pulled out the telescopic sight. Lying full length he cradled the carbine butt against his shoulder.

A young face flashed into the circle of glass. Down below it, the three white stars of a British captain. Perhaps a company commander or assistant company commander, Stuermer told himself, knowing that in such a class-conscious nation as the British, the men were helpless once there were no officers to give them orders. He exhaled slowly and squeezed the trigger. The rifle butt recoiled against his tensed shoulder.

For a long time the young Captain stood motionless in his tracks, while the khaki line flooded about him. His face appeared shocked and contorted in the telescopic sight. Suddenly he jack-knifed and pitched to the ground violently.

The brutal-faced NCO next to him stared down in consternation at the dead officer, just as Stuermer fired again. As the NCO opened his mouth to call out an order, the slug caught him in the stomach and punched him off his feet. The British line came to an awkward stop.

Stuermer, feeling no pleasure in what he had just done, lowered his rifle. 'Try to keep them at that distance – and watch those carriers . . .'

A sudden burst of vicious automatic fire whined off the boulders behind the foxhole in a series of murderous ricochets.

'All right, stand by everywhere!' Major Greul called out, as a small group of men, sheltered by one of the little bren carriers broke to the left and scurried for the next patch of cover on the battle-littered slope. 'Here they come!'

Everywhere along the German perimeter men opened fire. The second battle of Mount Clidi had begun!

Ox-Jo looked at the corpse from which stretched an apparent endless length of intestine like a marker tape. 'Well, he's not leaving for one. The poor bugger!'

Jap, busy with fitting out the mules which would take the Stormtroop's wounded out, grunted: 'Come over here and give me a hand.'

'What's up?' Ox-Jo growled and ducked automatically as a Tommy slug slammed into the other side of the bullet-ripped shed which housed the mules. 'I thought you were the expert muleskinner?' In thirty minutes they were due to evacuate the mountain and Jap wanted to have the mules, awkward creatures at the best of times, fully ready. 'Now this is what I want you to do. I'm going to put the harness on this ugly brute in a minute and you know what he's gonna do? The bastard, awkward as he is, is going to inflate his stomach. Once I've got the harness on, he'll let the air out of his guts so that the harness will hang there loose and I'll have to do it all again.'

Ox-Jo thrust out a thick lower lip in a gesture of admiration. 'Smart buggers, aren't they?'

'Now this is what I want you to do. As soon as I lay the harness on him and he starts his little tricks, I want you to plant a swift kick with your dice-beaker right up his arse. That'll surprise him and he will let go of the air in his guts.'

'And what if he kicks back?' Ox-Jo protested.

'Be hard luck on you, Ox. Then you wouldn't be bothering the girls in the knocking shops on payday any more.'

As Jap slipped the harness on, Ox-Jo landed a tremendous kick against the mule's rear. It whinnied piteously, but released the air in its belly. Jap completed the task of saddling him without any further difficulty. Rapidly he passed down the lines of mules fixing their harnesses with expert ease, Ox-Jo assisting with well-aimed blows to the animals' rears when they threatened to be obstinate. Finally he was finished. 'All right, Ox, trot off and report to the Colonel that we can start loading the wounded now.'

Colonel Stuermer fired his last flare. The green light soared into the air and coloured the faces of the handful of men still holding the perimeter a sickly hue. They responded to the signal immediately. They opened up with everything they had. A furious hail of tracer slashed the darkness to their front where the Tommies had begun working their way up the steep slope. Stuermer raised his hand. The waiting men tensed. The troopers holding each mule laden with a wounded man, clasped their hands reassuringly over the animals' muzzles.

'All right, Corporal, off you go. We'll give you exactly five minutes and then we'll start the diversion.'

'Good sir,' Jap spun. 'All right, you mule-skinners start 'em off.' One by one, as the green signal flare faded over the top of the mountain, the sure-footed mules with their cargo of wounded left the perimeter.

Stuermer beckoned Greul and Meier, who made up the headquarters party which would be in the lead, and strode to the edge of the perimeter. He raised his carbine. '*Storm-troop Edelweiss*,' he cried at the top of his voice, '*follow me!*' He darted forward. The men streamed after him, firing as they ran. In the chaos the English troops could not see who was friend, who was foe. They held their fire until it was too late.

The mountaineers were among them, slashing and slamming their carbine butts into the crouching men, bayoneting without mercy. Within minutes they had opened up a path through the British line, sending the Buffs reeling back on both sides to allow the mule train through.

Five minutes later they had disappeared for good, leaving Mount Clidi behind them, abandoned, and occupied only by the dead.

FOUR

It was a strange night full of alarms and excursions. Fire fights seemed to be going on on all sides. From the sea too came the sound of battle and unidentifiable aircraft seemed everywhere in the dark sky. Twice they ran into British positions and fought their way through them. There was no sign of the Green Devils, however.

The hours passed in a back-breaking nightmare, as they stumbled up and down steep slopes, tripping and falling time and time again on the boulder-studded, scree-covered hillsides.

Half an hour later, the weary men of Stormtroop Edelweiss did finally 'get lucky'. It was three in the morning when, as they stumbled up a treacherous slope in single file, they heard the hoarse croak-croak of the paras signal – a bullfrog decoy – that Colonel Stuermer had been waiting for all night.

He pressed the five pfennig device he held in his hand hurriedly.

It was answered by the same croak-croak and a cautious voice called from somewhere in the darkness, 'Stormtroop Edelweiss?'

'Yes, Stormtroop Edelweiss here. You the Fourth Para?'

'Yes sir – and are we glad to see you mountain boys!'

'Well, we are delighted to see you Bavarians, Colonel Stuermer!' Baron von Waldstein said with unusual animation as they crouched together over the map in the candle-lit cave which was his HQ.

'Not as glad as we are to see you, Major,' Stuermer breathed. 'I had begun to think that I was walking on my knee stumps instead of my feet.'

'I know the feeling well, my dear Colonel,' the Baron

laughed sympathetically. 'But shall we apply ourselves to the situation at hand?'

'Certainly. But don't expect me to think very straight for a start. It has been a hell of a day!'

'Mein lieber Herr Oberst,' the Baron replied, 'it has been a hell of a war. I have not been able to think straight since Eben Emael in forty*. But no matter. Let me fill you in.'

'Please.'

'Well, General Mueller is already landing troops at Parteni Bay in the north and Pandeli Bay just below Leros. Just before my radio was knocked out, I was informed by Mueller's HQ that the Parteni landing was in trouble. The Tommies had delivered a very strong counterattack and there was every likelihood that our people had been thrown back into the sea.'

Stuermer frowned. 'And the landing at Pandeli?'

'Apparently there we managed to get ashore and form a bridgehead. That was at zero three hundred hours this morning.' Stuermer bent and peered at the map, his shadow wavering on the wall as the breeze made the candle-flame dance.

'That means,' he said after a few moments' consideration, 'that once the Tommies realize that we no longer hold Mount Clidi, they are free to attack Rachi Ridge from the north. There is nothing to tie them down there.'

'Exactly. We've got what I estimate is a battalion massing against us for a dawn attack to the south from the direction of Mount Meraviglia and those two companies you mentioned, Colonel, and perhaps the men now freed from the Parteni landing in the north. In other words, they have us from front and rear. Decidedly unpleasant, what?' Baron von Waldstein gave one of his unnerving laughs. Stuermer disregarded it. All he knew was that the Baron, who looked like a caricature of the typical chinless, aristocratic Prussian officer, was a good man to have at his side at this particular moment. Nothing seemed to scare him.

*A surprise German para-attack on the Belgian fort at Eben-Emael which took place in 1940.

Stuermer pondered for a moment or two. Outside, the guns had begun to thunder again. Soon it would be dawn and on the British side of the line, officers like himself, tired, strained and overworked, would be planning their moves on the deadly chessboard of war. 'You said that the landing at Pandeli Bay had been successful, Baron?' Stuermer asked suddenly.

'At zero three hundred yes.'

Stuermer frowned at the map. 'There are two things we can do now. We can sit up here in a good defensive position, growing callouses on our backsides waiting for the Tommies to attack us, while their comrades deal with the Pandeli Bay landing at their leisure.'

'That was General Mueller's original plan, Colonel. We have the mission of keeping the British forces split until there are sufficient seaborne troops available on Leros for an all-out attack on Mount Meraviglia.'

'But Mueller, with all due respect, is a big-footed stubble-hopper whereas you are a para and I'm a member of the High Alpine Corps, Baron.' Stuermer forced a grin. 'We don't do things like the infantry do.'

'No, we disobey orders and chance getting ourselves courtmartialled, providing we live that long! Do what—?'

'Launch a two-pronged attack on their HQ at Mount Meraviglia, with the seaborne forces coming in from Pandeli Bay to form the other prong.'

'Oh, my God! That's really, crazy, Colonel!' Baron von Waldstein cried. But there was still a grin on his face.

'Why bother about wasting time on the *guts* – the rest of the island. Let's go for the *head* right from the start, *their HQ*. Once that is destroyed, I can assure you the Tommies will pack up. I've seen it happen time and time again in the past.'

'I'll believe you, Colonel. But I hope you'll tell the presiding officer your theory loud and clear at my court-martial. And when do we start?'

'At dawn, Baron and this is how we're going to do it.' Urgently he leaned across the map and began to explain . . .

130

FIVE

'In the name of the blessed Saint Patrick!' – the Fusilier on outpost duty caught himself, and overcoming his surprise at seeing a civvie mule train appear suddenly out of one of the Ridge's many gullies, called : 'Halt! Who goes there?'

The first civvie, a wizened little man with a kind of towelling turban wrapped around his head and a blanket flung over his ragged khaki shirt in the island fashion, tugged at his mule's bit cruelly and jerked it to a stop.

'Did you come from up there?' the Irish sentry asked, gesturing with his rifle at the Ridge top.

The little man shrugged, as if he did not understand. The other two – a hulking brute of a man and a horse-faced, smaller one – did the same.

'*Milate anglika?*' the sentry asked.

The little one shrugged again as the horse-faced Greek growled '*ochi*'.

'Great balls of fire!' the sentry cursed. 'If you don't speak English—' he stopped short. 'Hey, what've you got in those panniers?' he dug the muzzle of his rifle in the first basket slung on the leading mule's back. 'Booze?' He licked his parched lips in an elaborate gesture of being thirsty. '*Ouzo . . . krasi . . . bira?*' He looked expectantly at them, his total knowledge of Greek exhausted.

The horse-faced man wagged his dirty finger across his face in the Greek gesture for no. '*Ochi . . . milo . . . achladi rodakino.*'*

'Bloody wogs!' The sentry hesitated for a minute. The civilians looked harmless enough, even though they had come from the Jerry positions. But it had been the same when the Battalion had been in Africa; the wogs had always been wandering around the battlefield, ignoring the shit

*'No, apple, pear, peach.'

131

flying everywhere, seeing what they could scrounge. 'All right,' he waved his rifle at them. 'On your way!'

'*Efcharisto,*' the horse-faced one said. '*Moulari!*'* He gave his mule a tremendous whack to set it in motion again. Slowly the little train of mules passed through the line, heading apparently for the slope of Mount Meraviglia. Then they disappeared from sight round the next bend, leaving a neat pile of steaming droppings right in front of the sentry's foxhole.

Baron von Waldstein hitched up his turban – a para sweatrag – and breathed out hard. 'The advantages of a classical education, Corporal,' he chuckled, 'and three months on Crete in forty-one, mending a broken leg.'

'Don't know about that, sir,' Jap said, threading his way through the boulder-strewn valley, enjoying the heady, herb-scented air of an Aegean dawn. 'I nearly shat in my britches when it looked as if that Tommy was going to check the panniers.'

'Well, you chaps,' the Baron said, reaching for his monocle and then thinking better of it, 'let's get on with this war!' He whacked his mule over its broad grey rump and dodged out of the way hastily. 'All right you filthy beast, giddiup!'

Operation Trojan Horse had entered phase two.

With his binoculars carefully shaded so that the sun did not reflect upon their lenses, Colonel Stuermer watched the Baron's slow progress through the Tommy lines. Then he swung round and scanned the whole area to his front.

To his right in the far distance was Leros. He could see the white and blue houses of the little town sparkling in the sun, and the curved scimitar of the Turkish coast beyond.

It was a breath-taking panorama – the majestic beauty of a Greek island at dawn, with the air full of the scent of wild mint and honeysuckle and pine – but it beguiled

*Thank you, Mule!

Stuermer for only an instant. He concentrated on the task ahead.

He swept his binoculars to the left, until they came to rest on the centre of the British defences – Mount Meraviglia. The Tommies, as lazy as always about digging in, had only constructed shallow holes and gun-pits and their positions were to be seen clearly. But if they were shallow, they were nevertheless numerous.

Slowly he surveyed the Mount's slope – pock-marked with the craters of the German bombs. The HQ itself would be the log-roofed bunker, with the wireless aerials gleaming in the sun above it. All around it were the trenches of the infantry. That would be the HQ's defence platoon. He ran his glasses down the rows of anti-aircraft machine-guns and the dug-in 25 pounder gun until they fixed on the battery of 3.7 inch Bofors.

Their lean barrels were pointing upwards, waiting for the next German air-raid, and Stuermer could see tiny black figures toiling all around them, filling more sandbags to replace those destroyed in the night's raids. There were four of them, ideally placed, for the Germans, on a little height which was almost parallel with the British HQ.

Stuermer lowered his binoculars. He knew the Bofors. The neutral Swedes, eager for earnings, allowed it to be built under licence by both the British and the Germans. But whereas the British only used the high velocity cannon in an anti-aircraft role, the German Army had also discovered that it could be used as a very effective infantry weapon, when nothing else was available. Time and time again in Russia, *Luftwaffe* flak gunners had turned their big cannon down to protect hard-pressed infantrymen against the attacking Russian hordes.

If they could capture those guns, they could use them to blast hell out of the Tommies, presently occupied in preparing all-out attack on Rachi Ridge below. More importantly the Bofors dominated the Tommy HQ. They would be able to use the site as a spring board for a final attack on it. First they had to capture the guns.

He rose to his feet and doubled back to their own positions where Major Greul was waiting for him impatiently.

'Well sir?'

'They got through all right.'

'Thank God,' Greul breathed a sigh of relief. 'We and the paras have about twenty wounded capable of using a weapon.'

'Hm, not enough to make the Tommies down there think we're still manning the Ridge in full strength.'

'I've already taken care of that, sir,' Greul retorted buskly.

'How?'

'I've had a whip round for spare clothes and blankets, and I've ordered the paras to surrender their jump helmets.'

'Why Greul?'

'Because I want to make dummies, sir,' Greul answered, obviously proud of himself and his ingenuity. 'Then we'll place the dummies in every second foxhole. At that distance the Tommies won't be able to make them out. Everyone knows that the British have no stomach for close-quarter combat.'

'Excellent, Greul. A good idea! That should fool them – for a while at least. How long will it take?'

Greul pointed to the squatting paras and mountaineers, busy stuffing grass and twigs into blankets and shirts. 'Perhaps another fifteen minutes. Half an hour at the most, sir.'

Stuermer did a quick calculation. By that time the Trojan Horse (the Baron had picked the name for their little deception himself) would be in position next to the Bofors, providing that the three of them were not discovered or stopped by some officious Tommy sentry.

'All right, Greul, speed up the men the best you can. I want those who remain behind to start this little diversion as soon as they're finished. Then we must see that we get down there and support the Baron.'

Stuermer stared up at the rock face that they would have to scale if they were to escape from the Ridge without being spotted by the Tommies below. 'It's not going to be easy with those paras attached to us. Though I suppose in their job they must have a head for heights.'

'I've already thought of that, sir,' Greul said. 'I'm assigning one of our chaps to each paratrooper. Our men will be able to help them over the more difficult bits. There will be no problems.'

No problems? Stuermer felt like shouting out in exasperation. He had never before been confronted with an operation with so many built-in problems. Here he was trying to fool a sizeable enemy force that his position was being held in strength, when in truth it was being defended by a handful of wounded. If that were not enough, he was going to lead a bunch of novices up a tricky climb in the hope that if they managed to scale the height, three men – the Baron, Meier and Jap – would be able to ensure that they were not greeted by a blast of 3.7 fire.

But instead of shouting, he contented himself with commenting passively: 'All right, Greul, carry on, please.'

Operation Trojan Horse had entered phase three.

SIX

'Now I want you paras to listen carefully to what I have to say,' Colonel Stuermer said slowly, noting the looks of apprehension on the soldiers' tough faces as they stared up at the eighty metre rock wall. 'There is nothing to be afraid of except fear itself. You will ascend by a rope that I have selected personally and which I personally will fix at the top of this height. When you ascend, there will be a trained climber in front of you and one behind. Fear will make you freeze and if you freeze you – and our whole force probably too – will be lost. Speed is the keynote to the success of this climb.' He let his words sink in, running his eyes gravely over their suddenly pale faces. 'Now any questions?'

'Yes sir,' a hoarse-voiced para sergeant said. 'Do you think I could get a quick transfer to the Quartermaster Corps, sir?' the NCO asked.

His sally broke the tension. Laughing the men started to stream forward to the rock face. Behind them the wounded took up their weapons and prepared to fire.

As their first ragged volley crashed out, Colonel Stuermer began his lone climb, a thick coil of rope slung over his shoulder.

The first twenty metres were easy, but then his luck started to run out. Holds were few and in a couple of instances, he had to resort to a pinch-grip, gripping a small nose of rock between thumb and finger, in order to be able to move on. Once he hung on solely by means of a hand jam, his fist slotted into a hole, his muscles screaming out in agony as he cursed and sweated in his attempt to drive in a spike with his free hand, the whole weight of his body supported by his fist.

But he pressed on, knowing that time was of the essence, ignoring the burning agony of his strained muscles, moving on steadily, using every technique he knew to speed up the climb. Then he was stopped dead. The last ten metres or so was an over-hanging mantleshelf of rock.

'Shit!' he gasped angrily. Pitches of that kind were difficult enough at the best of times, but under the conditions they faced now! Not only would he be searching for hand-holds, he would be fighting gravity, with his body stretched precariously over the rockface at an angle of forty-five degrees.

Grimly he reached up and thrust his right hand in the pocket hold and jammed his knee against the rock. He grunted and reached his left hand upwards to take hold of the jug he had spotted just above him at about a metre's distance. Now supported by his right hand and knee, he hung fifty metres above the ground, with his body tilted at an impossible angle.

He had almost reached the jughold with his left hand

136

when disaster struck. His right knee slipped. In a flash he was swinging in a frightening, dizzying arc, connected to the mountainside solely by his right hand. Somehow or other, his right hand held on. Perhaps it was the excruciating pain which ran like fire through his hand and arm, which kept grip on the rock. He repressed the desire to scream and fought back.

Summoning up all his strength, tautening the muscles of his stomach and lower back, he swung himself forward violently. His boots crashed against the rock face. But his left hand found no hold. An instant later he was sailing out into space again, catching a wild glimpse of pale, strained faces staring upwards at him.

Sobbing for breath, the muscles in his right shoulder ablaze, Stuermer forced himself to try again. He couldn't hold on much longer. 'Now!' he cried and swung himself forward once more. His left hand scraped against a jagged edge of rock. Desperately he attempted to seize it. The rock ripped his frantic fingers. The blood rushed out and they slipped.

Stuermer attempted to calm himself. He had stopped swinging away from the rock now. He controlled his thudding heart and drew a deep breath. It was now or never! If he did not make it this time, he would have to let go. His right shoulder muscles could only stand another few seconds of the intolerable strain.

Suddenly Stuermer was detached and calm. He had always known he would die on a mountain. Ever since he had taken up the challenge of the 'German Mountain' in the faraway Himalayas, he had thought he might well die on Nanga Parbat. Now it seemed he would meet his end on this insignificant slab of rock, not even dignified by a name.

'All right,' he thought, 'one last time!'

With the last of his strength he swung himself up to the rock face again. His frenzied fingers caught and seized the bloody spur of rock. *They held! This time they held!*

Five minutes later he had hauled himself over the lip

of the mantleshelf and had thrown himself full length on the cropped grass, sobbing for breath.

'Hey what yer up to, wog?' the sweating gunner asked, looking up from the sandbag he was filling and staring at the strange procession of mules and the even stranger-looking civvies leading them. 'Don't yer know there's a war on?' With a jerk of his head he indicated the firing coming from Rachi Ridge.

'No spik Engleesh good,' the Baron ventured in what he hoped sounded like Greek-English. 'You like firewater?'

The gunner jerked upright. 'What did you say?'

Hastily the Baron opened a pannier and pulled out the flask of brandy, which was presented to all paras when they went into action. There had been a lot of ominous muttering from his Green Devils when he had asked those who had still not emptied their flasks to hand them over. He held it up for the English soldier to see. 'Brandy,' he said, 'German brandy.'

'Where did you get it from?' the gunner asked suspiciously.

'There,' the Baron indicated the Ridge, 'Many Germans – dead.'

'Cor stone the fucking crows!' the gunner exclaimed. 'You wogs are right old tea-leaves. You even rob the dead.' Still there was a light of interest in his eyes. 'What do you want for it?'

'You corned beef?' the Baron said.

'Bully! Heaps of it. The old Kate Karney lives off bully. How much?'

The Baron held up one finger. '*Ena*'. Then he thought better of it and held up two fingers. '*Dio.*'

'Two. Come off it,' the soldier said scornfully. 'I could have that booze and your old woman thrown in with it too for two tins of bully. One!'

The Baron, enjoying his role now, spat coarsely in the dust at the soldier's feet and shrugging, said. 'Good – one corned beef. You bring?'

'Yes, I bring. Now you just wait there, and if you've got any more of them flasks for sale, my mates'll buy them. After last bloody night, we can do with a drink.' The soldier dropped his shovel, all thought of work forgotten now, and hurried over to a little wooden shed in the centre of the emplacement. Obviously it was the little battery's ration store.

'Quick!' the Baron snapped, very business-like now. While the Baron in his role of Greek pedlar beamed at the back of the departed gunner, Ox-Jo and the Jap went to work. Covered from observation by the mules' bodies, they pulled out the plastic explosive from the panniers, and thrust the ten minute time pencils into the soft substance. Within seconds, they had ten one pound lumps of the explosive ready. Swiftly they tossed the explosive into the great piles of shells which were stacked ready for the next attack some fifty metres from the guns. With luck the shells would explode and cause the necessary diversion, without harming the guns themselves.

There was no time for any further considerations: the eager gunners were already streaming back holding up their tins of corned beef, crying 'Lead us to it, wog! . . . Where's all that lovely booze?' and a sweating Baron was handing out little metal flasks in all directions. Operation Trojan Horse was about to enter its final phase!

'It is better to explain to your friends why you cheated on a climb than to explain to St Peter why you didn't,' Colonel Stuermer had told himself, using the old climbers' motto; and had lied accordingly to the apprehensive paras. They had believed that what had happened on the over-hanging mantleshelf had not been dangerous but part of preparing the ascent for them. Reluctantly they had begun the climb and surprisingly enough it had gone without incident.

Now they were winding their way down the steep edge of the Ridge adjacent to the sea. The beach below was deserted, as Stuermer had anticipated it would be. The Tommies, hadn't enough men to cover everything. Now the para-mountain force could swing inland again behind the Tommies hidden by the fold in the Ridge.

Stuermer dropped the last few metres to the valley floor and looked at the beach behind him. It was clear. He looked ahead. Nothing, save the burning olive groves, dotted here and there by a white peasant cottage, the heat-waves already rippling over the tiles in a hazy-blue shimmer. Behind him man after man dropped to the ground.

'All right,' he barked. 'At the double now!'

From the direction of the Fortress HQ came the first of the explosions he had been expecting for the last five minutes, followed instantly by a mushroom of black smoke hurrying into the perfect sky. The Baron had pulled it off!

'Come on,' Colonel Stuermer yelled. 'Let's go!' He began to double towards the hill, which was now being rocked by explosion after explosion.

SEVEN

As the last charge exploded, Ox-Jo pressed the trigger of his machine-pistol. The two Tommy gunners stopped running and went down, jerking, spinning, collapsing. Another handful of survivors fled the destruction and ran straight into the fire of the three Germans crouched in the ditch beyond the battery.

The last shells erupted in a rush of noise and flame. Debris and bits of bodies flew into the scarlet sky. Then the noise stopped and Ox-Jo stared at Jap in dazed shock, knocked speechless by the ear-shattering proximity of the explosions.

The Baron took his finger off the trigger of his machine-pistol. The frenetic stammering stopped at last. The sudden silence, broken only by the crackle of the flames, seemed oppressive; even louder than that which had just gone before. Then von Waldstein jammed his monocle in his eye

140

and cried: 'Come on, let's see what's happened to the guns!'

They needed no urging. Across the Fortress HQ, there was complete confusion: whistles blowing shrilly, officers and NCOs bellowing orders, the roar of motorcycle engines bursting into sudden life. The three men ran through the fire, springing over the terribly mutilated bodies of the Tommy gunners, pushing aside the burning debris to get to the gunpits.

The first gun was useless. The heap of shells had been too close and its long barrel was twisted into a knot. But the other three were still intact, apart from the fact that the paint on their barrels was blistered and bubbling from the intense heat.

'You cover us, Jap,' the Baron shouted. 'We'll try to get the first one operational for the rest of the force. They should be here in a couple of minutes.'

Swinging themselves into the twin seats of the first ack-ack gun, the two of them started to twirl the brass handles furiously to bring its muzzle down and direct it at the Fortress HQ, from which uncertain machine-gunfire was beginning to wing its way in their direction.

As Jap ripped off a wild volley over the valley, the first paras and mountain troopers came running into the battery positions. 'As slick as owl shit,' he thought. 'Trust old Stormtroop Edelweiss!'

That afternoon Colonel French's Irish Fusiliers swung round from their positions at the foot of Rachi Ridge and began their attack on the Germans who had appeared so suddenly to their rear. But the Fusiliers didn't get far. The *Luftwaffe* Messerschmitts and Stukas, summoned up by radio, came in time and time again. At tree-top height they zoomed in, machine-guns and cannon blazing. In the end the frustrated French had temporarily called off his attack and set his mortar platoon to soften up the mixed para-mountaineer force, knowing that on the stony hillside a bursting mortar bomb was ten times more murderous than normal.

Now a bare-headed French, blood dripping from a deep wound in his forehead, crouched behind the cover of a large boulder, calling Tilney on the radio.

'Listen Tilney, I want all the artillery fire you've got after dusk, once we've got rid of these damned Jerry fighters. You must support us with everything you've got. Give them a good fifteen minutes and then we'll go in.'

'But French, the Boche are landing in real force at Pandeli Bay! They already hold Leros and are moving inland. I've got to think about stopping them too.'

'Tilney,' French cried in exasperation. 'Must I repeat myself? Concentration is everything. First we must get rid of this cancer on our own back. With the Buffs, who are working their way over the Ridge, we can then launch an all-out attack on the Pandeli Bay Germans. Concentrate, Tilney, *concentrate*!'

'Easier said than done, French,' Tilney's voice came back over the air, metallic, distorted, but definitely angry too. 'What with the Boche coming up from the sea and those of yours down there, pounding us with those captured Bofors, it's not exactly a garden of bloody roses for us up here either, you know.'

Next to French the MO prepared to deal with the next in the long line of casualties. French gasped in horror. It was young Charley O'Kane, his arm shattered, bright red blood jetting from it as if from a wide-open tap. Tilney heard the gasp. 'What is it?'

'Oh, nothing . . . casualties.'

'Are they bad?' Tilney asked, his voice softer now.

'Pretty. At a rough guess my companies are down to half strength. But we're still capable of dealing with the Jerries down here, as long as you give us the necessary artillery cover.'

'All right! At dusk, let us say,' he consulted an aide, 'at eighteen hundred hours. But I can't give you more than five minutes. I daren't take my twenty-five pounder fire

142

off the Boche on the other side of Fortress HQ for longer than that. They might have some idea of a night attack themselves. You understand?'

'I understand, Tilney.' He gritted his teeth. Next to him the MO was beginning to snip through the ragged flesh of O'Kane's arm with a horrible, sickening sound, while the young Captain attempted to stifle his moans; they had run out of dope now! 'Five minutes will be enough for my Fusiliers . Thank you.'

'The best of luck, French . . .'

'All right, lads, on your feet!' French commanded, as the guns above them thundered and the twenty-five pounder shells began to crash down on the Bofors battery.

Everywhere the survivors of the Royal Irish Fusiliers rose to a crouched position, their bayonets gleaming a dull silver in the dusk. French nodded his head in silent approval. His Paddies weren't going to let him down.

He glanced at the glowing dial of his watch. Four minutes to go till the end of the barrage. He would give the guns two more minutes. It would take them 90 seconds to cover the hundred yards between them and the German positions. He would have to risk losing a few men through 'shorts', as he had to be at the German perimeter before the guns ceased firing.

'Stand to!' French shouted above the roar of the guns. He gripped his revolver more firmly in a hand that was damp with sweat. The Bofors firing at the Fortress HQ had now stopped their pounding. Obviously their crews had gone to ground. It was a good sign. French raised his revolver. 'Royal Irish Fusiliers,' he cried. 'At the double now!'

The four hundred odd survivors of the First Battalion started at an awkward jog, stumbling here and there in the darkness over the bodies littering the slope, but keeping formation, their bayonets held in front of them determinedly, ready for the fight to come. *Seventy yards . . . fifty yards . . . forty . . .* French felt confident they would

143

make it now before the barrage lifted. Then his Paddies would take care of the Germans. Their blood was up. It would be a massacre. *Thirty yards*.

'They've come far enough!' Colonel Stuermer cried above the roar of the barrage, the shrapnel whining off the rocks all around. He lifted his carbine and trying to ignore the danger about him, aimed it at the ragged line of Tommies, slipping and stumbling on the slope below. 'FIRE!' The German perimeter burst into life, drowning even the dying roar of the Tommy barrage, catching the enemy at point-blank range. It was not war, but sheer suicide. At that range they could not miss. The first line of Tommies was swept away instantly, as if scythed down by some invisible reaper. Still their comrades of the second line came stumbling on. Fighting back the wave of revulsion that threatened to overcome him, Colonel Stuermer aimed and fired again.

The Fusiliers had been cut down to little groups, stumbling blindly forward through the confused noise and smoke to their lonely deaths.

A Fusilier with a crimson farmboy face tried to mount the boulder which formed the corner of the German perimeter, a satchel of hand grenades slung over his shoulder. The enemy fire mowed him down just as he reached the top. Another Fusilier grabbed the bag from the dying man and attempted the same climb. A burst tore his stomach out. Colonel French, his revolver gone, grabbed the bag. Without a glance at what was left of his shattered Battalion, he cried crazily, 'Follow me, the Irish!'

He ran at the rock. A slug struck him in the shoulder. He staggered, but did not seem to notice. Behind him the handful of shaken survivors began the ascent, as if they were eager to die.

French surmounted the boulder. He reached into the bag. Another bullet struck him, low in the belly. He gasped with the incredible pain of it, and went down on his knees, tracer zipping through the night in his direction. He pulled out the grenade. With fingers that felt as thick and clumsy as sausages, he tugged at the pin. It seemed to take a terribly long time to come out. Something buffeted him in the shoulder. He didn't notice. His whole attention was concentrated on the metal ring. 'Bash on, Irish' . . . Just as he managed to pull it out, a last burst swept him clean off the boulder. He was dead before he hit the ground below, littered with the bodies of his 'Paddies'.

Colonel Maurice French was dead and the First Battalion Royal Irish Fusiliers existed no longer.

'*Cease fire . . . cease fire!*' Colonel Stuermer cried urgently. Allowing the hot carbine to fall from his nerveless fingers, he stared hypnotically at the handful of survivors, wounded all of them, hobbling painfully and silently like sleepwalkers down the slope littered with the bodies of their comrades.

'They'll never come again,' Greul crouching next to Stuermer in the foxhole said, and even his arrogant voice was tinged with something akin to awe.

EIGHT

All that night, while Stuermer's Bofors fired round after round into the Fortress HQ, General Mueller pressed home his attack on Leros. At dawn the *Luftwaffe* came winging in at full force to deal with the last of the British anti-aircraft guns. One by one they bombed them out of action. Now the *Luftwaffe* dominated the sky.

Desperately Tilney requested GHQ for naval support. Three destroyers steamed into Alinda Bay, but harassed by continual German air attacks, their barrage fell, not on the German positions there, but on the Buffs attempting to clear Rachi Ridge. In the end the destroyers withdrew hastily, chased by Stukas, their shattered decks littered with wounded.

General Mueller started to put in more and more troops, his sea landings now virtually unopposed. By the evening of 15 November, Mueller had twice as many men on the island as Tilney.

Tilney's new plan had been to contain the Germans on the coastal strip around Alinda Bay, before he threw them off the island altogether by means of a counter-attack. Now as one alarming report of German landings followed another, he knew he did not have the men to mount a counter-attack of that kind.

GHQ radioed that he should withdraw the Buffs from north to south by sea. But there were no boats to be found, the Buffs' CO was dead and most of his company commanders wounded; the younger officers now in command were barely holding their own as it was.

Communications between the British units began to break down. The radio link with the Buffs went altogether. The only way to reach them was by runner and there weren't many volunteers for that virtually suicidal task. The British were gradually being forced into isolated pockets, hard-pressed by the triumphant Germans.

Yet in spite of the seriousness of the position, Colonel Tilney's determination to hold out to the last did not waver. Casualties in the Fortress HQ were still relatively light, his troop of 25 pounders were still in action with plenty of ammunition, and in the way of infantry he had the most resolute and experienced troops still available on the island – a large detachment of Jellicoe's Special Boat Service. As that terrible 15 November drew to its close, Tilney addressed his assembled officers : 'Gentlemen, there must be no talk of surrender. We have a good position here. We stick it out until the gentlemen of GHQ come up with some means of rescuing us,' he hesitated for a mere fraction of a second, *'or we fight to the end*! Is that absolutely clear?'

'Sir!' as one the assembled officers clicked to attention, prior to leaving again for their posts, while outside the 25 pounders began to thunder once more . . . Colonel Stuermer

146

clapped his hands around the Baron's ear and yelled above the roar of the guns, 'Baron, I've about had a bellyful of this.'

'That makes two of us, Colonel. What do you suggest we do about it?'

'The Tommies are well dug in and equipped up there and Mueller's chaps seem to have no pepper in their pants. They're not making much progress. The way things are at present, those damn Tommies out there could hold out like this for ever.' Stuermer nodded. 'You see that projection over the Tommies' command post – just beyond the aerials, Baron?'

'Yes.'

'If we could get a few determined men down that, they'd be right on top of the command post. A couple of grenades and the way would be open. It might be the quickest and cheapest way of ending this whole damned business.'

'A few determined men,' von Waldstein said. 'You make it all sound easy – damned easy, Colonel. But have you forgotten that the Tommies up there are as thick as fleas on one of those mules' backs. Let them catch you hanging on up there – and I could imagine your determined men would be singing castrati pretty rapidly.'

'I'm counting on the darkness and the general state of confusion to cover us.'

The Baron looked at the outline of the bunker and the height above it, suddenly revealed in all its danger by a stab of scarlet flame. 'Do you think I could decline this particular waltz? I'm afraid I haven't got much of a head for heights.'

Stuermer clapped him on the shoulder. 'No, Baron, I don't want you on this one.\ You will take charge of the battery here. I'm taking only my most skilled men on this one.' He rose, his decision made, and cupped his hands around his mouth. '*Major Greul . . . Sergeant-Major Meier . . . Corporal Madad . . .* over here, at the double, please!'

It was nearly one o'clock on the morning of 16 November,

1943. The 25 pounders located around the Fortress HQ were still thumping away in defence of the position, but the volume of fire had diminished. In spite of both the defenders and attackers' weariness, red, white, green signal flares zipping into the dark sky everywhere indicated that no one slept, and it seemed to Colonel Stuermer, as he and the other three slipped cautiously through the wire, that the darkness was full of tense, expectant men, waiting for the daring little party to make its first wrong move. An icy finger of fear traced its way down the small of his back and he shuddered.

'Anything wrong, sir?' Ox-Jo enquired.

'No, just keep that wooden eye of yours open, Meier. The Tommies seem to be everywhere.'

'Not surprised, sir, seeing we're almost in the middle of their camp now.' He took a hold of his CO's arm and pointed at the dark outline of a gun. 'One of their 25 pounders. Wouldn't be too healthy to continue in that direction.'

As silently as they could, the four of them slipped back into shadows and turned right. The Tommies did not see them. Time passed. Once a patrol came within five metres of them and they pressed their bodies against a rough stone wall, their hearts thudding so painfully that it seemed the Tommies had to hear them.

They nearly bumped into the sentry. Just in time the soft smoker's cough and the red glow of a half-concealed cigarette in the darkness warned them of his presence. Greul doubled forward, crouched low. The sentry never knew what hit him. Greul reached up and pulled hard. The sentry's flat soup-bowl helmet slid backwards. Greul grunted, and thrusting his knee into the small of the man's back, tugged with all his strength. Joyously, Major Greul garrotted the sentry to death, the chin strap biting deeper into his soft throat. Finally he was satisfied. He relaxed his hold. 'He's dead,' he whispered and let the body slip to the ground. 'Come on . . . all clear, now.'

Then they reached their objective above the command

post. 'Thirty metres or more,' Stuermer whispered. 'What do you think, Greul?'

'Yes, it'll be about that.'

In silence two of the world's greatest climbers stared down at the overhang, assessing the difficulties as best they could in the dim light, while Jap and Ox-Jo looked at the pale blur of their faces like two patients waiting for some great doctor's verdict – life or death.

'VS,' Stuermer said, only half-joking.

'Very severe classification? Agreed,' Greul said seriously. 'Hard climb, needing lightweight footwear, strength and skill. Sometimes well nigh impossible in poor weather conditions,' he rattled off the textbook definition easily.

Stuermer intervened : 'Now there are only two real problems to this descent. One we can't really see what we're about. Two—'

'If the Tommies down there spot us before we've got down,' Jap interrupted quickly, 'we're gonna get an awful – er – headache.'

'Right you are, Madad. All the more reason for getting down it as quickly as possible, and as silently.' Stuermer pulled the rope off his shoulder. 'I'm going to rope you down and you're going down without your boots on. Without your boots you'll be silent and be able to find the smallest toeholds, the only kind of purchase we'll find this face.'

'Great stacks of shit,' Ox-Jo cursed, as he bent down and began unlacing his boots. 'What a life this is ! Now I'm going to have to fight the war in my bare feet like a sodding ballet-dancer !'

NINE

His body tingled with expectancy, Stuermer braced himself to take the strain. He sensed fear-laced excitement, for he was going to rope down the others – *abseiling* – with

149

himself as the belay. In that darkness they had been unable to find any suitable outcrop of rock to anchor the rope. It was going to be a terrible physical strain. But it was the only way.

'Sir, don't you think you ought to let me be the anchor.' It was Meier. 'They always said I was built like a brick shit house.'

'You have it, Meier,' Stuermer said. 'You might have the strength, but I've got the skill – and I've got to get down without the aid of the rope.' That settled it. The fundamental system was to loop the rope over a firm spike of rock to act as an anchor and let the climbers slide down a double rope, controlling their speed by friction. It was quick, but it was dangerous – Stuermer could think of a dozen professional climbers who had been killed while roping down. However speed now was of the essence and Stuermer was determined to take any reasonable risk to get his little team down to the command bunker.

Meier lowered himself over the side of the rockface. Colonel Stuermer thrust his legs apart and took the strain. 'All right, sir,' Meier gasped, 'I'm off!'

The rope quivered. Stuermer braced himself. The weight of Meier's massive body transmitted by the rope almost dragged him from his perch, but he did not call to the others to support him. They had enough on their hands preparing to descend. A metallic slap and Meier gasped with pain as his stockinged feet hit the rock face for the first time before he took off for the second bound.

Slap and gasp. Meier had completed his second bounce. Perhaps two more to go and he would be down. Stuermer held on grimly, his breath coming in rasping gasps, his body lathered in sweat in spite of the night cold. Suddenly the pressure relaxed. The rope was down. 'Thank God,' Stuermer whispered to himself and relaxed, shaking his burning hands to restore circulation.

Greul stepped forward, boots slung around his neck by their laces.

'Ready, sir. Are you sure that—'

150

'Don't even talk about it, Greul,' Stuermer muttered through gritted teeth.

Greul adjusted the sling and went over the side without another word.

It seemed to take him an age to clamber down the steep face, and the strain on Stuermer's back was intolerable. Just as he felt he could stand it no longer and would have to let go, the weight on the rope relaxed. Greul was on the ground also.

Stuermer leaned weakly against an anxious Jap, dizzy and breathless, his pain-racked hands trembling violently.

'Sir, give up,' Jap urged. 'Let me have a crack at going down without the rope. I think I could pull it off.'

Stuermer shook his head numbly. 'Not experienced enough . . . go . . . now!' The words were forced out through his teeth in staccato gasps. How he managed to hold the little Corporal, Stuermer never knew. His face ashen and wild-eyed, he held on, praying and praying that he would not let go. And then Jap had released himself, dropping the last few metres blind, knowing that the CO was at the end of his tether. Stuermer was on his knees in the grass, his arms dangling at his side, his head bent in mute supplication, oblivious of time and place.

Eventually he managed to pull himself out of his trance and began the climb. It was a nightmare. Time and time again he took suicidal risks in the pitch darkness. Later when he came to view the virtually sheer drop, he shuddered and told himself that only a crazy man would dare tackle a climb like that at night. But he fought his way down, hanging on by his fingertips, his toes bruised and bleeding, feeling for the slightest hold.

And then, out of the eternity of that night, Greul's voice said softly : 'You're about five metres from the ground, sir. Let go – we'll hold you.'

With a sigh of blessed relief the Colonel let go, his eyes closed, as if he wanted to shut out the pain-dominated world for good. He dropped – right into Ox-Jo's brawny arms.

They were on the mound of packed earth, which formed part of the left wall of the bunker. The command post was virtually impregnable. Stuermer sized up their position quickly, as they listened to the muffled sounds of the staff working – unaware of their presence – somewhere deep below.

'What are we going to do, Colonel?' Greul asked urgently. 'It's clear we can't tunnel our way through this lot.' He indicated the thick mound.

'No.'

'Go through the front door?' Ox-Jo suggested facetiously.

'In a way, but not the front door exactly.'

'What do you mean?' Greul whispered.

'Well, we all know these stable headquarters. They start off with only the simplest design. But in slack periods, to keep the men busy, fresh excavations are started and in the end you have a whole rabbit-warren of a place underground. So if we can't use the front door, we must find another entrance. There must be one.'

'I can tell you where you'll find it,' Jap said. 'Every time some soft-handed clerk gets taken short, you can't have him rushing through the front entrance to the thunderboxes. Well, sir. I know where the latrines are. My guess is we'll find the other door there.'

Jap was right. A thin crack of yellow light split the darkness of the other wall of the bunker, and there was only one sentry guarding the door.

Stuermer advanced boldly towards the man, whistling the only British tune he knew – *Tipperary* – and fumbling with his jacket, as if he was returning from the latrines.

'Pipe down!' the sentry hissed. 'Don't you sodding well know—'

'Look left!' Stuermer cried urgently.

The sentry fell for the old trick. Alarmed, he swung round. Ox-Jo loomed up out of the darkness to his right. The earth-filled sock struck the sentry at the base of his neck, just below the helmet. He went out without a sound. Stuermer caught him just in time. Carefully he lowered

152

him to the ground. Major Gruel and Jap hauled him deeper into the shadows. The way inside the bunker was open.

The tunnel ahead of them – cut out of the naked rock, its floor covered by duckboards – was empty, lit by a couple of naked bulbs strung roughly along its ceiling. But there seemed something threatening about the tunnel's very emptiness. Stuermer fought back the desire to turn and run while he still had chance. Instead, he gripped the machine-pistol more firmly in his hands and padded forward, followed by the others.

There was an opening cut in the rock wall to their left, covered with a blanket. Stuermer nodded swiftly to Greul. He threw the curtain aside, as Stuermer stood there, legs astride, machine-pistol at the ready, finger curled round its trigger.

But the soldiers who filled the room presented no danger to the four invaders. They were dead. They lay in neat rows, rigid, motionless and unseeing, exactly as if they had died on parade instead of bloody battle.

'Must have been a casualty clearing station,' Greul whispered, unmoved.

They pressed on to the left. Heavy snores were coming from the next room like those made by wounded men, their pain killed by massive sedation. With a wave of his hand, Stuermer indicated they should bear right, reasoning that the Tommy commander would not want his operations room directly next to the casualty clearing station.

They padded up the corridor to yet another blanket-covered door. From within came the subdued buzz of voices. Again Stuermer took up his stance and indicated that Greul should prepare to pull back the curtain. *'Now!'* he rasped and went in, machine-pistol blazing.

An officer – an elderly man with grey hair – dropped to his knees, a line of red holes stitched neatly across his chest. Another officer was flung round by the impact at that short range and smashed into the rock wall, his bloody fingers scraping a red trail on it in his dying agony. A third's face exploded in a welter of blood and shattered

153

bone. Suddenly everything was panic-stricken confusion: orders, counter-orders, cries of rage and fear, wild bursts of firing.

A couple of Tommies in their underwear came running down the corridor. Greul felled them with a quick burst. More followed, skidding to an abrupt stop and crumpling to the ground, as the Schmeissers caught them. Something struck Stuermer's hand a terrific blow. He yelped with pain. The Schmeisser dropped from his nerveless fingers. A figure in khaki slid from behind the dying elderly officer. The Tommy clasped a big revolver, attached by a white cord to his neck. He raised it. At that range he could not miss. Stuermer could see every last detail of his crimson, angry face, down to the blackheads around his eyes, as he started to squeeze the trigger.

Stuermer catapulted forward. The whole weight of his lean body hit the Tommy in a murderous tackle. His shoulder rammed the officer below the breast bone. The revolver jerked upwards. The bullet struck the ceiling harmlessly and the officer went down.

Next moment the two of them were rolling on the dusty floor, locked in a desperate fight for survival, hands clasped around each other's throats, while all around them staff officers and the orderlies broke down the Stormtroop Edelweiss men's resistance, sacrificing themselves almost eagerly to eradicate this deadly threat. And then a heavy brass rifle butt smashed into the back of Colonel Stuermer's skull and just before the black wave of unconsciousness swamped him, he realized they had bitten off too much. They had failed. Now they were the Tommies' prisoners.

TEN

Stuermer forced himself out of the void and opened his eyes, hearing the first words in English, 'But, my God,

Colonel Tilney, he's a full Colonel! They must be confident if they're sending such men on suicide missions like this.'

Stuermer moved his head and groaned. A wave of red-hot pain swelled through his skull and he closed his eyes momentarily, just as the officer who had been speaking bent down to him.

'You speak English?' he demanded.

'Where are my men?' Stuermer asked hoarsely, opening his eyes once more and staring up at the unknown faces all around him.

'They are our prisoners – they are all right,' the unknown officer said slowly and superciliously. Stuermer guessed that he would be the unit's intelligence officer. 'Thank you,' Stuermer said. 'Could I have a drink of water, please?' A younger officer, with an unshaven face and a blood-stained bandage around his head poured some water from a jug into a cracked enamel mug and handed it to their prisoner.

Stuermer took his time. The officer's first remarks had given him an idea. The fact that he, a colonel, was involved in what appeared to be a commando raid, obviously indicated to them that the German Command was supremely confident that the British were finished and that they were prepared to take almost suicidal risks to hasten the inevitable defeat.

The men around him were at the end of their tether. It only needed the right phrase, perhaps even only a single word, to nudge them over that fine line between renewed hope and black despair. As Stuermer finished the water and handed the mug back to the aide, he determined that he would nudge the three Tommies across that very line.

They talked deep into the night. Stuermer had never realized just how much English he remembered from school and his expeditions in India. He worked incessantly on the three Tommies, telling them tremendous lies about the size of the German forces on the island and the miserable state of Tilney's scattered, cut-off units.

155

For what seemed hours, Colonel Tilney rejected his every claim with muttered grunts of 'rubbish' and 'quite impossible'. Still Stuermer worked on him knowing that the Tommy Commander would break in the end.

At five o'clock a fresh batch of wounded were brought past the open door of the operations room. 'Dawn hate, sir,' a weary, tousled doctor said almost casually.

Tilney recognized one of his company commanders – his right leg streaming with blood, held to the thigh by a piece of shrapnel-riddled flesh. 'My God,' he gasped, sickened by it all, 'they're slaughtering us!'

Then Stuermer knew he had the British Colonel. He was a commander with too much sensitivity: a fatal weakness in a soldier. He had fought the same weakness in himself often enough and knew it well; in battle, one had to close one's mind to the sufferings of others, if one wanted to avoid being paralysed by compassion.

'Colonel,' he cried urgently, 'why continue this bloody business? You have fought bravely against overwhelming odds. You have done everything up to now. But if you continue,' he shrugged eloquently, as if he were too much of a gentleman to say more.

'What do you mean, Colonel?' Tilney asked sharply.

'If you continue the result will remain the same. We shall win! But you will sacrifice your men – for nothing. You will sentence your men to death unnecessarily. They will call you the butcher of Mount Meraviglia.' Stuermer broke off, letting his words sink in.

Tilney's grey face revealed the emotions that were conflicting within him at that moment, fighting each other for control : concern for his men, his injured pride, dejection, hope for a miracle, the awareness that his whole military career might well be finished if he surrendered to the enemy. This was the year of victory in the Middle East. Prime Minister Churchill could be ruthless with commanders who let him down in 1943, especially if the surrender of Leros meant the end of his hopes to recruit Turkey to the Allied cause.

156

Suddenly his shoulders slumped, as if he could not tolerate the iniquitous load on them any longer. 'All right, you win,' he said weakly.

'But sir!' the aide protested. The Intelligence Officer silenced him with a swift glance. 'What do you want me to do sir?'

It seemed to take Colonel Tilney a long time to answer, but when he spoke his words were dry, precise and completely unemotional. 'Contact Lieutenant-General Mueller's HQ. Tell him, I am prepared to negotiate the surrender of Leros ...'

Down below the surrender negotiations dragged on and on at interminable length. But Colonel Stuermer was no longer interested; he was drained of every last emotion and unutterably weary. He sat on the roof of the bunker in which the talks were taking place, ignoring his own troopers and the paras who were wandering curiously through the British positions, treating the still-armed Tommies with cautious respect.

Stuermer's eyes were fixed solely on the landscape of death and destruction which stretched as far as he could see. Shattered, blackened trucks, a wrecked bren carrier, rifles thrust downwards with helmets hanging from their butts, the markers for the graves of the fallen; and everywhere in the wire, the bodies of the night's dead, hanging on the strands like abandoned bundles of rags.

'Stuermer,' General Mueller's harsh voice broke into his reverie. Reluctantly he rose to his feet and turned wearily to face the General.

Mueller's eyes gleamed with triumph. 'They have surrendered, Stuermer!' he cried enthusiastically. 'Leros is ours – thanks to you and your men ... Do you understand, Colonel? *Leros is German!*'

'Yes sir, I understand.' Without even saluting, Colonel Stuermer turned and began to stagger down the steep slope of the bunker like a drunken man. It was all over.

ENVOI

The khaki-clad crocodile shuffled wearily down the dusty road towards the waiting boats. Dejected British prisoners-of-war being taken from Leros to the Greek mainland to spend the rest of the war behind barbed wire. Nearly five thousand of them, officers and men, victims of bad planning, over-confidence and a political manœuvre which had failed.

Baron von Waldstein, no emotion visible on his face, wrinkled his nose at the stench which came from them as they shuffled by the little waterfront *taverna*. He raised his glass of ice-cold *ouzo* and drank from it quickly.

Leaning against the wall of the inn, considering the beaten men not as enemies but as human beings like himself, defeated by the same harsh fate, Colonel Stuermer asked softly, 'What's the matter, Major? Can't you take the smell?'

The Baron shrugged. 'It is a bit high, Colonel. But then the poor chaps haven't had much time for their ablutions these last few days, I suppose.'

'You'd do well to get used to it, Baron,' Stuermer said slowly. 'It is the smell of defeat. You will be smelling it often enough in the months to come.'

Baron von Waldstein eyed the tall mountaineer, with his right arm in a sling, his lean face revealing the strain of these last few days all too clearly. 'Anything wrong, Stuermer?'

'Not much. Mueller has just told me the Allies have broken through in the mountains.'

'In Italy?'

'Yes,' Stuermer answered tonelessly, his mind obviously preoccupied with new problems.

'May I venture to guess that you are going there?' the

Baron said carefully. 'To a place called Cassino – Monte Cassino?'

'Yes. Apparently it is the back-up position for the whole Italian front.' Stuermer finished the last of his *ouzo*, and prepared to leave. Major Greul was signalling to him from the deck of *Korvettenkapitan* Doerr's S-boat. 'Why do you ask, Baron?'

Baron von Waldstein smiled softly. 'I received a signal from Papa Student* this very morning that after my Green Devils have been reinforced and re-equipped in Greece, we are to be sent to Italy – to Monte Cassino to be exact.'

'Then we shall meet again.' He extended his left hand. 'Left comes from the heart, Baron,' he said, sudden warmth in his voice.

'So, they say.' The Baron took Stuermer's hand and pressed it hard. 'Yes, we shall meet again. Good-bye, sir.'

'Good-bye, Baron.'

Without another word, Colonel Stuermer turned and strode purposefully to the waiting S-boat. 'All right, Doerr,' he commanded, 'take her away!'

Doerr rapped out an order. The S-boat's big diesels surged into wild life. Trailing a long, seething ribbon of white behind it, the S-boat moved out of the little harbour.

Hastily Sergeant-Major Meier, his big body festooned with looted British cameras, clutched the rail and steadied himself. He tipped the bottle of English whisky to his lips, his broad face suddenly very green. Swiftly he swallowed a great slug, the fiery spirit spilling out of the bottle and running down his unshaven chin. 'Jap,' he moaned, 'I think I'm gonna be sick!'

Jap caught the bottle neatly before it hit the heaving deck. 'The pride of the High Alpine Corps – *I've shat 'em*!' he said in mock contempt, and then as the S-boat hit the open sea and his own stomach began to rumble ominously, the little Corporal took a hefty swallow of the looted whisky and prepared himself for the long voyage ahead.

*General Student, head of the German paratroops.

Behind them the little island, which had seen so much horror and death these last days, began to grow smaller. Standing next to Doerr, feeling the salt breeze slap him in the face, Colonel Stuermer did not look back. He wanted to forget Leros and what had happend there. He tried to focus his mind on that remote mountain in the Himalayas, that white-gleaming, defiant peak which he dreamed of conquering.

As Leros finally vanished on the horizon, Stuermer stared across the surface of the gleaming stretch of sea ahead, as if he could already see what lay awaiting them in that remote, mysterious distance – more death and destruction. STORMTROOP EDELWEISS WAS GOING TO THE WARS AGAIN!